PRAISE FOR

when i was broken

"A beautiful reminder that sometimes life doesn't go according to plan . . . An incredible tale of love lost and found . . . A real life story labeled as fiction . . . A must read!"

Sherri Lewis, Essence Bestselling Author of "My Soul Cries Out" and "Selling My Soul"

"WHEN I WAS BROKEN is so compellingly real that I found myself repeatedly stepping out of editor mode and reading ahead. What I couldn't wait to see on those beautifully articulated pages was not just whether and how brokenness would be fixed, but the essential truth that love does indeed conquer all that is not love."

Jo-Ann Langseth, Editor

"WHEN I WAS BROKEN is inspiring and heart wrenching – filled with love, friendship, loss, and renewal. I commend the author for bringing such an honest and gripping story to light, and for giving voice to so many who never told their stories."

Maiysha Clairborne MD, Author of "Eat Your Disease Away"

"Imani's writing is as refreshing as her presence. An encounter with either is proof that she is chosen to change lives. Her energy and spirit are boundless, being courageous enough to live and spiritual enough to share her experiences."

Jay White, Author of "Tap Into Your Destiny"

"WHEN I WAS BROKEN is a beautifully written first novel from an extraordinarily gifted author we are sure to see more of for many years to come. . . . This book pulls you in early on; from the moment you realize that this just as easily could have happened to you."

Travis Hunter, Bestselling Author of "The Hearts of Men"

this book is dedicated to love

PROLOGUE

Dear God,

Today was a really bad day. It all started when they came to my house and almost took me away. I don't remember much of what happened before they arrived – only that a man seemed to suddenly appear and begin calling my name.

"Mrs. Bennett? Ma'am, are you ok?"

The words gradually pierced through the fog that enveloped my brain. As no more than a reflex, my eyes slowly opened just wide enough to focus on what looked like a uniform. Police? Why were the police in my bedroom? Now, only slightly curious, I opened my eyes a little wider and looked cautiously upward at the officer's thick neck, then a little farther to his brown, moon-shaped face. No, I didn't know him. Nor did I want to know him.

Finally, I realized that the police had come because we called them. Or rather, because my husband, Marcus, called them when he found me lying on the bedroom floor, crying hysterically. Best I could remember, I had gotten down on my knees to pray, then found myself simply unable to get up. I was so incredibly tired. I just didn't feel like doing it anymore. It was as if all that had happened in the past few months had finally become too much. As if the weight of it had crushed my spirit to pieces and I no longer had the strength or desire to try to put them back together again.

So there I was, lying on the floor of the bedroom, with the phone up to my ear, listening to the psycho-babblings of a counselor Marcus had called after hanging up on 911. I couldn't process most of her words, but her shrill tone – which she probably thought was soothing – caught my attention periodically. She spoke quickly and methodically, not even seeming to care if I was still on the line.

While I listened to her voice, the officer and my husband whispered softly back and forth, every so often glancing at me. The way they disregarded my presence made me feel like a child being shunned from grown folks' business. Little did they know that I couldn't have cared less what they were saying and that I might not even have been able to comprehend it if I tried.

Meanwhile, the counselor was telling me all the reasons why she couldn't see me that day. The last thing I heard her say was, "We can get you in for an appointment on Monday."

My brain moved slowly, trying to decipher her words. They came to me as if through a haze or from some faraway place. What day was it? I couldn't quite grasp it. Had I gone to work that day? *No, not today. Yesterday? Yes, I think so.* My mind focused momentarily, fixating on the present. That meant it was Saturday. Then comes Sunday . . . then Monday. Monday was two days away.

Two days away? What would I do with an appointment two days away? By then, it would be too late. She just didn't get it. I was all out of options.

"I want to come in today and I want to stay at the hospital!" I said, hoping she'd hear the desperation in my voice. I couldn't explain further, but surely she would hear my need. *Didn't she know that I couldn't make it two more days? I couldn't even stand two more minutes!* My eyes pooled again with tears. My heart began to race faster.

"Well, Angela, since you're not suicidal, there's no need for you to come in today. Today we can talk about what's bothering you by phone, and then we'll get you in for a visit on Monday."

She said this as if her lines were scripted and rehearsed. I might as well have been talking to a recording.

I heard screaming inside my head, but I don't think I uttered a sound – surely not an intelligible response. Gripping the phone as if it were my last lifeline, I sank to the floor and curled into myself like a caterpillar trying to get back into its cocoon. All I could see ahead was a sea of darkness. The only sound I heard was my own pounding heartbeat. Heaviness compressed my chest and oppressed my soul, causing me to feel as if the walls were closing in. As if I was falling into a deep abyss. *Maybe if I just let go, it would all be over soon. Maybe, I thought, I could just will myself out of existence.* Was that a suicidal thought? Would they take me now?

Marcus must have explained to the policeman that I was talking to a counselor because the next thing I knew, the officer bent down and gently pried the phone from my fingers. He spoke hurriedly into the receiver, saying little, as if trying to conceal the other end of the discussion. Worse than that, he kept looking at me and smiling like an idiot – as if hoping to soothe the crazy woman who was lying on the floor, crying hysterically.

I wanted to pull the officer aside and make him understand. *My husband has lost his mind! My entire world and everything I thought to be true is a lie.* The words formed in my head, then quickly froze on the tip of my tongue as I caught sight of Marcus out of the corner of my eye. He was standing arrogantly in the doorway. I took in his worried expression. Hand on his hip in a staged posture of concern. Well-tailored navy slacks with white dress shirt, still crisp from the cleaners. Signature cuff links, manicured nails, and a clean-shaven head. He looked perfectly normal. He looked stable. He looked like a man in control. Only I, who knew him almost as well as I knew myself, because I'd known him for more than a decade, could detect the subtle emptiness in his eyes.

But me? Rising above and looking down, I saw myself as if for the first time. I wore cutoff sweatpants and a raggedy t-shirt that had seen better days. The clothes, while meant to be loose, hung without the slightest form because of all the weight I'd lost within the past few months. I still wasn't slender by conventional standards because I had the classic black woman's hips, but anyone who knew me could see that I had easily dropped a dress size or two. I had no bra on to contain my small breasts, and my short, usually stylish hair was uncombed and badly in need of a perm. No makeup and red, puffy eyes added to my disheveled appearance. And, as if that weren't bad enough, I had folded my five-foot, nine-inch frame into a fetal position on the floor beside the bed. Attempting to block out everything, I lay there with eyes that probably looked as if they'd seen death, and welcomed it. I lay there, unquestionably and irreparably broken.

My breath caught sharply as a startling thought slowly formed in my mind and almost caused me to gasp out loud.

I looked like the crazy one.

PART I

"Falling Apart"

1

"I DON'T KNOW HOW TO DO THIS."

We have been sitting for what seems like hours, but has probably been only a few minutes, and I am already regretting my decision to come. My eyes quickly dart towards the door a few feet away, as I wonder how to grab my coat and make a quick run for it.

"Do what?" Mary asks.

"You know . . . talk . . . about what happened."

The mere thought brings tears to my eyes, but I refuse to let them win this time. If I focus hard enough, I can push the tears back where they came from, with all the rest. I've actually become quite good at this over the past few months. Much better than I would have imagined.

"Ok," Mary says as if it is settled. "Well, then what do you want to talk about?"

Instead of answering, I take a minute to look around Mary's office, noting how different it is from what I expected. Unlike a typical counseling office, this feels more like somebody's living room. Somehow Mary has managed to cram an oversized love seat, a recliner, a small coffee table, and three bookshelves into her office. Yet, the room doesn't feel cluttered. I glance over at the space heater in the corner, which is no match for the December chill. Finally, I check out the bookshelf, taking in the book titles and the angel figurines that adorn more than one shelf.

God said he's going to bring you to a place of brokenness, I think, but say nothing.

"Ah, I see you like my angels," she says. "I know some folks might think I shouldn't have them in an office, but they make me feel safe. Know what I mean?"

I attempt to smile in response, but somehow the signals must get crossed because darn if that tear doesn't find its way out instead. I ignore the box of tissue in easy reach.

"I guess it's not really the figurines; it's more of what they represent," Mary says, as if we are having a two-sided conversation. "I'm one of those people who believes that there's something higher in control. Some master plan that we're all part of."

"I used to believe that," I say, attempting to sound more composed than I feel.

"Used to, huh? So, what do you believe now?"

Nothing, I open my mouth to say, then shut it again because that isn't true.

"I don't know. It's just hard for me to believe that God would —"

"—let bad things happen?" Mary finishes.

I nod my head and lean forward to grab a tissue. Just one, as if in some subconscious desire to be under quota for the day. Mary says nothing, likely waiting to see if I keep talking. I don't.

Am I really ready to share how my life fell apart without warning? How I am struggling with every molecule to fix it, but not even sure where to begin?

Mary smiles and nods at me, as if in answer to my questions. She is probably no older than my mother, but something about her feels grandmotherly, like she might give me some hot chocolate and make it all better. If only it could be that easy.

4

"So, Angela, what if I tell you a little bit about how I work, then we can see where to go from there?" Mary asks, then settles back into her reclining chair.

"Ok," I finally respond softly. I wonder where my voice has gone. Where the strong woman I know has disappeared to, replaced by this quiet shell that now sees the world for what it is: a place where people lose things they love every day.

In that moment, I really look at Mary – noting her kind features and Afrocentric look, complete with beautiful silver locks and a head wrap. Her intense gaze tells me that not much gets past her, while a steady smile conveys that she can be trusted. I imagine she knows what it's like to have the world turn on you.

"Have you been to counseling before?"

"Only a couple of marriage counseling sessions with my husband," I say. My husband. The man who has driven me crazy. I think about how he called 911 a few days before, but decide it's not worth mentioning.

"Ok, then let me start by telling you what you won't get here. I know a lot of my patients have watched Dr. Phil and folks like that, then they come in expecting me to give them answers. But, that's not how this works. I believe you already have the answers, and it's my job to help you find them . . . . Ok?" Mary squints her eyes as she looks at me intently.

"Ok." I still feel practically mute, but am comforted when Mary gives me a warm smile as if to say, "See, you already found one answer. Let's see what else you can come up with."

"So . . ." Mary says, in a way that sounds more like a full statement than the start of a question, "are you ready to tell me what brings you here today?"

I pause a millisecond, as I contemplate where to start. It has only been a few months since everything started, but lives have been created and lost in far less time.

"It's me . . . and my husband, Marcus. . . . It wasn't supposed to be like this. . . .I just don't know if I can do it anymore."

I pause for the tears, but they don't come, which gives me a misplaced sense of satisfaction. Perhaps I am better today or perhaps I have removed myself from this time and place, as I often do now.

"Ok," Mary says. "Well, that's a start. Are you ready to tell me about it?"

I'm not sure if it is Mary's voice – which sounds like it can melt marshmallows – or the way she leans back in the chair as if we have all the time in the world, but suddenly I want nothing more than to tell this woman everything.

I take a deep breath, hold it, and then begin to exhale my story.

2

I T WAS A DAY LIKE ANY OTHER.

Marcus kissed the back of her neck. When she didn't respond, he kissed her again, this time lingering as he tasted the skin behind her ear. His breath tickled her eardrum, but still she didn't move.

He didn't either. His hand found the familiar resting place where her waist gave way to the hips she'd finally stopped trying to exercise away. Not because of the way Marcus looked as if he'd lost his best friend every time she made real progress, but because she'd finally accepted that resistance was futile.

His hand traced the path from her hip to her thigh and came back to rest in its easy chair. It was a route he knew well, and a morning routine that Angela could have scripted. The sequence sometimes moved around – a touch before the kiss, three kisses instead of two — but the play was mostly the same.

They would remain in a spoon position until their breathing synchronized and became one. It was their way of making sure to take a moment to stop time and just be together. It was their way of conveying, "Good morning. I missed you last night; I'll miss you today" without ever saying a word.

Minutes would pass with them lying there quietly, until they could no longer put off the start of another day. Then, one of them would finally break the hold to signal that it was time to get up and get moving. As silly as it was, Angela liked to be the one to move away first. Although she couldn't have explained why, his pulling back first always made her feel somewhat vulnerable. Maybe it was because Angela wanted to pretend that she was in control – that she needed Marcus less than he needed her.

"Baby, it's time to get up," Marcus said, rising up just enough for her to feel cool air rush in under their blanket. "If you press snooze one more time, you'll have to get dressed in the car."

She wanted to throw a tantrum like a three-year-old. *No-o-o-o-o, I don't wanna get up!* Instead, she rolled onto Marcus' chest and tried to absorb a little bit of his energy, while reminding herself that there was only one more day to get through before Friday. Sad that she had only been working at the law firm for two months and was already living for Friday.

"Angie? You awake?" Marcus caressed her cheek with a tenderness that made her feel fragile and precious.

"Just ten more minutes" was her intended response, but it likely wasn't intelligible as she pulled one of the pillows over her head and tried to ignore the relentless beeping sounds that started up again from the alarm clock on their nightstand. She was doing a pretty good job at it until kids yelling outside started to compete with the noise. Something about the first week of school always made them extra rowdy.

Angela touched her stomach gingerly, then smiled to herself. She pulled the pillow from her head and leaned farther into Marcus. Almost as if in a choreographed scene, her lips found his though her eyes had yet to open.

Marcus allowed his fingertips to continue their exploration. They moved down past her lips and neck . . . down, up, and back down to the center of her chest . . . then farther to the bare skin just south of her silver belly ring. With his index finger, he drew circles on her stomach and watched her squirm involuntarily at his teasing.

Then, just as quickly as it began, the music stopped. Without warning or explanation, Marcus' caresses ended with a light pat on her thigh.

"You better get moving. It's almost eight," he said, finally leaning over to turn off the clock.

A number of responses came to mind, but he was right. She was late. Again. To a job where she should still be trying to make an especially good impression. She tried to shake away the last remnants of sleep, and told her slightly aroused body that night loving was just as good as morning loving, and there was plenty of time for that later.

On the other hand, tonight was a really long time away.

"Sweetie, I'm going to start the shower. . . . Come with me?" Angela teased, then slowly moved away from his embrace, and eased her legs over the side of the bed.

For some reason, as her bare feet touched the carpeted floor, she hesitated before going farther. Looking behind her, she took in Marcus' six-foot, three-inch frame stretched across the ebony bed. His dark brown skin was in stark contrast to the cream satin sheets and comforter. The lines on his brow had grown into a full tree, seemingly overnight, and his eyes were no longer those of the starry-eyed junior who'd bumped into her on campus eleven years before. He wasn't the same as when they met, but Angela could honestly say that she loved him even more than when they first started dating. Even more than when she married him almost five years ago.

Something beyond words tugged at her — made Angela want to crawl back into the bed, wrap her arms around Marcus, and try to stop time. Just hold him there in the moment for as long as it would last. Not worry about being the strong one or pulling away first. Just call into work and stay home, where everything was right.

But instead of following her gut, she shook it off. Just get through today and tomorrow, and we'll have the weekend. Plenty of time to lie in bed all day on Saturday.

Walking into the master bath, she turned on the shower to let it get nice and steamy while she brushed her teeth on her side of the double vanity.

"Marcus, the water's r-e-a-d-y!" she yelled into the room moments later. Hearing no response, she stepped back into their bedroom to see what was taking him so long. Her eyes flitted from the laundry basket of towels next to the window, past the bookshelf and armoire, to the unmade bed. The room was empty. At that moment she heard sounds of the shower running in the guest bathroom down the hall. Angela swallowed her disappointment and resisted the urge to invade his space.

After quickly showering and throwing on a cream-colored pantsuit, somewhere between frying a few curls into her Halle-Berry-like short hairdo, Angela daydreamed about a life that didn't involve alarm clocks and billable hours. By the time she'd finished applying a little eyeliner to frame her light brown, almond-shaped eyes, gloss to accent her full lips, and powder to take the shine off of her caramel skin, she was no closer to figuring it all out.

She could hear Marcus downstairs in the kitchen, humming a tune she'd never heard before. Since their second car was in the shop, Marcus planned to drive her in to work.

"Baby, you ready?" Angela asked as her feet touched the bottom step.

"I've been ready," Marcus responded curtly, walking ahead of her toward the door.

Angela started to say something to try to thaw his chilled tone, but decided against it. In truth, Marcus was a morning person and was rarely late for anything. On the other hand, Angela feared she was really a vampire in disguise since she loved to stay up at night, and absolutely hated to get up in the morning – especially for work. So, his waiting on her wasn't exactly atypical.

Climbing into their black SUV, Angela sighed deeply when she saw that the clock on the dash read 8:45.

"Sweetie, I'm gonna have to work late tonight to finish the memo I told you about," she said to him. "Especially since I'm going in so late."

"Ok." Marcus' eyes didn't leave the road.

"I don't know why I'm making this so hard. It's not like this is something I haven't done before. It's just . . ." Angela continued to gesture with her hands as she paused to try to put her feelings into words. "It's just I'm really nervous about turning in my first big project. You know?"

"Umm-hmm."

"I guess I just want it to be really, really good so they'll know they hired the right person." Angela looked over at Marcus again, her eyes pleading for him to understand. Much to her dismay, he still didn't return her gaze.

Getting no response, she continued. "Cuz you know how these law firms are – you don't have much time to prove yourself. If they think you're not gonna make it, they'll fire you in a minute.

"Of course, they don't call it firing you, but it's the same thing. They ask you to leave and you're stuck trying to explain why you left a job after only two months. Not trying to go out like that."

"Yeah," Marcus mumbled absentmindedly, as he signaled to get onto I-20, which would lead them directly into the heart of Atlanta.

"You feel me?"

"Ok," Marcus said, sounding as if he hadn't a clue what she was talking about. Angela tried unsuccessfully not to get annoyed that he wasn't really listening.

"Of course, if worse comes to worse, I can just – I don't know – maybe move to the islands and meet some nice Caribbean man who'll take care of me."

"Umm-hmm."

"Baby?" Angela exclaimed, her voice going up an octave.

"Huh?"

"What's up with you? You haven't heard a word I've said! I say I'm gonna move off with some man, and you say 'Oh, ok?' What's going on with you this morning?"

Taking his eyes briefly from the road, Marcus looked at Angela's pouting face and finally seemed to tune in.

"Angie, I'm sorry. I guess my mind was just somewhere else."

Angela stared at him expectantly with an expression that said "You're going to have to do better than that."

Reading her thoughts correctly, Marcus continued, "Look, I know going back to a law firm hasn't been easy. And, I hate the thought of you working at a job you don't like. But, I promise it's going to be worth it. Pretty soon, my business is going to take off and then you can do whatever you want."

Marcus turned his attention back to the road, then looked back at her quickly. "Except move off to an island with some guy, which would force me to kill somebody and go to jail," he added, the dimple in his left cheek deepening as he toyed with her. "Ok?" he asked, suddenly looking more serious.

"Yeah, ok," she replied, sighing inwardly. Angela felt bad for making him reassure her about a plan they'd both agreed was best. He'd been in the military while she was in law school. Then, she'd worked while he was in business school. After that, they'd more or less flipped a coin to decide who would be first to pursue their career dreams. Angela had always wanted to write a book, but since she really didn't know what she wanted to write about and had never even completed a short story, Marcus had won out. After his release from the military, he'd finished his MBA a few months earlier, then started his own company, connecting small businesses to government contracts. Angela had left her government job to take a higher-paying law firm job to support them in the meantime.

"Look, sweetie, I meant it when I said I believe in you, so you just keep doing your thing, and we'll be fine," Angela assured him. "Ok?"

Marcus gave her a half-smile, then turned his attention back to the highway. Taking his silence as a cue, Angela leaned her head back on the passenger seat and closed her eyes to enjoy the drive in from Stone Mountain to downtown Atlanta. With bumper-to-bumper traffic, she figured it would take close to an hour to get to the Peachtree Street exit.

It was 9:35 a.m. when they pulled up to the circular driveway in front of her building. Angela grabbed her briefcase from the backseat, climbed out of the SUV, and quickly walked around to the driver's side window. She stood there for a few moments before Marcus slowly lowered the window a little more than halfway, with a look of what appeared to be impatience.

"I'll call you later to let you know what time to pick me up," she said.

"Ok," he replied distractedly, as he shifted into drive and eased away from the curb.

Angela shrugged off the feeling that something was wrong. Knowing Marcus, he was probably off somewhere in his thoughts, dreaming about making his first million. Marcus had been planning to become the next Bill Gates since before they'd met.

As the truck began to pull away, she walked quickly to the revolving door of her office building, eager to get out of the August sun. Feeling that weird tugging sensation in her gut again, she turned back to wave good-bye one last time. But Marcus was already gone.

It was too late.

3

SOMETHING IS WRONG. **THOUGH SHE WAS ALONE IN HER** office, Angela had heard the words just as surely as if someone were standing there, screaming them into her ear. *Something is really, really wrong.*

The second time, Angela didn't so much hear the words as feel their portent, erupting deep inside. Felt it in the nervous fluttering of her stomach; felt it tingle all over her body. The feeling had been there, off and on, for much of the morning, but somehow she'd managed to push it into the background, putting everything else before it – until now.

Anyone who entered Angela's office probably would have assumed she had it all under control. Seated at her desk, files and treatises laid strategically in front of her, she wore the pensive look of a young attorney trying to meet a deadline. But after thirty minutes of switching "per your request" to "at your request" back to "per your request" in the first line of a memo, Angela pushed herself away from the keyboard and allowed her head to rest in her hands. Her memo wasn't going to get done until she started to focus, but for some reason it was hard to concentrate.

As the most recent lateral hire at the firm, and the only attorney at the firm to have graduated from a historically black college, Angela still had a lot to prove. Although it wasn't fair that she had to hold up the banner for an entire school – much less, for an entire race – Angela didn't want to give the partners at Wilburn & Bagley any reason to believe that Howard was any less than Harvard, or any other top-notch school. That's why she knew that her memo on indoor air-quality standards in Georgia had to be perfect. No typos or missing authority to make them question her skills.

God, are you listening? Please let me finish this memo tonight so that these folks will know that I can do this job. And, can you also please send me a sign that everything is ok?

Angela's prayers were interrupted by the ringing of her office line. She glanced quickly at the caller ID, then laughed out loud when she realized that it was Endia calling.

"Guurl, how'd you know?" Angela said as she picked up the phone.

"Know what?"

Angela laughed again.

"Never mind. Let's just say you've got reeeaaally good timing."

"Maybe I just felt you needed me," Endia said.

"Yeah, right. Sure that's what happened," Angela said, still somewhat unconvinced.

"So-o-o-o spill already!"

Angela opened her mouth, then shut it again as she considered her words. "I don't even know how to describe it, Endi. I've just had this weird feeling all day that something isn't right, but I can't figure out what it is."

"Well, has anything happened to throw you off balance? Something with Marcus? Or your family? Or work?"

Without even realizing what she was doing, Angela glanced at the mahogany bookshelf to her left, letting her eyes rest on the framed wedding picture that sat in the center. In the photo, Marcus and Angela both wore an incredulously joyous look that asked, "What did I do to deserve you?" in a way that still made her heart flutter. Next to it was her favorite photo of all time, with Marcus dressed in his white Air Force uniform, looking like he should be running for President.

"Well, both of us are a little anxious for Marcus' business to take off, but I think that's pretty normal.

"And, everything is good with my mom. I talked to her last night.

"What else did you ask me about? Oh yeah, work. Work is *different*. New people that I have to prove myself to. Still getting to know my way around. Of course, the hours are already crazy, but I knew what I was getting into when I came back to a firm, so I don't think that's stressing me."

What Angela didn't say was how anxious she was to get home and take a home pregnancy test. She could already imagine the look on Marcus' face when she told him that she was pregnant. But that should be making her feel happy. So why did she still feel like something was wrong?

"Well, if Marcus is good and you're good, what else could it be?"

"You know what? You're right. It's probably nothing," Angela said in a way that wasn't clear if she was convincing herself or Endia. "You know me. I'm always thinking too much."

"Hold on, hold on. Before you just discount everything, maybe you should sit with it a little more," Endia said. "Even though you're the most overanalyzing person I know —"

"Gee, thanks."

"You know what I mean. . . . You're a thinker. I get that." Endia paused before continuing. "But if you feel like something's wrong, that's different. You should listen to your intuition."

"My intuition, huh?" Angela said, laughing that she and Endia could continue having the same conversation year after year. It wasn't that she didn't believe in a sixth sense, she just hadn't had much luck with her own.

"Yes, your intuition. That little voice inside you that tells you when something's off. Don't ignore it. Listen and figure out what it's saying."

"I know, I know you're right. I promise to listen. . . . Anyway, enough about me, what's up with you? Did you get my message last night?"

"Yeah, girl, I'm sorry." Endia said. "Last night was the first time this week I've gotten any real sleep since we started shooting this commercial. I slept so hard I didn't even hear the phone. That's why I'm calling you now."

"Oh, when I didn't hear back from you, I thought maybe you decided to go out," Angela said, then in her most easygoing voice, added, "You know, someplace where you could maybe meet someone."

Angela felt the sigh even though she couldn't hear it through the receiver.

"Angie, please."

"What?" Angela asked innocently.

"Just let it go already. Please don't turn into one of those women who thinks everybody has to be married to be happy. I love what you and Marcus have. Kind of gives me hope it's out there. But, I'm good. Seriously."

"Ok, ok, I feel you. You're right. I just want you to be happy – whatever that means for you."

Softening, Endia said, "Yeah, yeah, I hear ya."

". . . Anyway, let me get off this phone and finish this work so I won't be here all night. Thanks as always for talking me off the ledge."

"Anytime. Call me back if you need to."

"Love you."

"Love you too."

Still smiling and feeling soothed by their talk, Angela turned back to the memo on her desktop. But within minutes, she was surprised to feel her stomach start doing flip-flops again. She tried to follow Endia's advice and just sit with it, but all she heard were the same cryptic words.

Something is really wrong.

4

"**A**NGELA, LET ME STOP YOU FOR A MOMENT."
Mary puts down her pen and paper to direct her full attention to me. "What made you think something was wrong?"

"I don't know."

"Are you sure?" Mary asks, leaning in closer, her voice just above a whisper.

I think back to the dream my mother shared with me a few weeks before everything happened, but I decide not to share. It's hard enough to think about what happened, let alone try to analyze whether this was somehow part of some cosmic plan.

I nod my head, hoping I look more convincing than I feel, then fold my arms across my chest, closing back into myself. I begin to block out Mary and all the things I'd rather not think about. My mind empties more easily now, choosing numbness over pain, time and time again.

"Do you need a break?" she asks.

It doesn't matter, I think. *There's no escaping*, I know. I avoid Mary's gaze. Something about her looking at me threatens to bring me back from my place of refuge. "Okay then, how about we switch gears for a moment? Why don't you tell me a little more background about you and Marcus? Something a little lighter."

The words penetrate. I breathe a sigh of relief. Someplace safe. I return.

"What do you want to know?"

I still cannot look at her, but I am at least back in this place.

"Whatever you want to tell me," Mary says. When my eyebrows rise, she adds, "How you met. How long you dated. About your sex life. . ."

"What?"

Mary laughs and holds up her hands in mock surrender, knowing she has broken through to me. "All I'm saying is tell me as much or as little as you're comfortable sharing. I want to understand a little more about you and him, before everything happened."

I uncross my arms and place them at my sides, willing my mind to remember what it was like before. My mouth twists in a way that is unfamiliar. It takes seconds for me to recognize that I am smiling, just a little, but enough for me to realize how long it has been since I felt happy.

"That's the thought I want," Mary says, smiling back at me.

"I was just thinking about when we met," I say. "Almost 11 years ago."

"How did you meet?" she asks.

"At Howard where I went for undergrad and law school. I was a sophomore, and he was a junior. I remember that it was December, because I'd just pledged a sorority."

"Go on."

"I was all excited – walking around campus in all this red and white paraphernalia. Random people kept stopping me to say congratulations. I was in my own little world, not really paying attention to anything as I crossed the street in front of my dorm. Suddenly, there he was, standing right in front of me, smiling like he'd just won the Super Bowl."

Mary leans back comfortably and I forget for a minute that we aren't two old friends at home, sharing a good story about a guy I like.

"His frat brother was talking – I think he introduced us, but honestly, I didn't hear a word cuz I was so struck by this guy – this guy with a smile that seemed contagious. He had – uhm, what's the word for it?" I stare at one of the angels on the table, as if it might respond. "Charisma? Nah, it was something more than that. It felt like he was holding a gigantic magnet, and it was pulling me toward him in a way that I couldn't – didn't want to resist.

"The next thing I know he was hugging me and congratulating me on pledging. I remember thinking that it should have been weird to hug a stranger, but the crazy thing is that it didn't feel weird at all. It felt like the most natural thing in the world. And, in that brief moment standing in the middle of the street on campus, completely oblivious to everything and everyone, I knew I'd met the perfect guy."

Mary jots down something on a notepad, then peers at me over her glasses. Her act reminds me that I'm not hanging out with a friend. I'm in therapy trying to make sense of what my life has become.

"So, was he all that he seemed to be?" Mary asks.

"What? What do you mean?" I place my arms back across my chest, but struggle not to close up again.

"You can interpret the question in whatever way you like. Just tell me what comes to mind first."

Was he what he seemed, I ask myself. I am quiet as I turn the question over in my mind, wishing for a different answer. When I finally run out of time on my internal clock, I look Mary in the eye.

"Well, was he?" Mary asks again more gently.

I take my time tasting the word as it tickles the back of my tongue, before being bold enough to move to my lips.

Finally, when I can delay no longer, I answer.

"No."

5

THE RINGING OF HER OFFICE PHONE STARTLED Angela, and stopped her from combing through the various things that could be making her feel so unlike her normal self.

"Angela Bennett," she answered briskly, without looking at the caller ID.

"Angela, it's me. I'm not far from your building. Can you come down?"

She glanced at the time on her computer and noticed that it was only 4:45. She'd been expecting Marcus to pick her up late that night. *Really* late that night. In her line of work, the day might just be getting off to a solid start at 5:00.

"Marcus, sweetie, it's early. I've got at least three more hours of work before I can get out of here, and that's if I actually focus instead of daydreaming like I've been doing for the past hour. I don't know what's wrong with me today –"

"Just come downstairs," he said. "I'll be there in fifteen minutes." Marcus hung up before she could respond.

Brow furrowed, Angela let out a deep sigh and hung up the phone, since talking to a dial tone wouldn't do much good. *Why was he in such a hurry?* He knew how much work she had to get done before the next day, and he knew how important it was for her to prove herself as the newest lateral associate at the firm.

As she reached for the phone to call him back and tell him he was tripping, another thought crossed her mind. Marcus never showed up unexpected at her job, or hung up the phone on her. In fact, his whole tone was really strange; it was as if he were hiding something. Maybe, just maybe, he had a little surprise for her? Maybe that's why she'd felt like something was off all day?

Angela's birthday was a few days away. Maybe it was an early birthday present. That's probably it. Marcus wanted to surprise Angela for her birthday!

With Marcus, you just never knew what to expect. For Valentine's Day, while he was still working as a consultant, he'd surprised her with beautiful diamond earrings despite her protest that it was way too grand a gift – especially compared to the jazz CD that she'd given him. Earlier that summer, he'd insisted that she go on a cruise to the Bahamas with Endia and Christine, even though they were on a strict budget because he'd quit his job to start the business and she wasn't making much money in her prior government position. And just a few weeks before, he'd surprised her by having a dozen of the most beautiful, long-stemmed red roses delivered to her office, for no occasion – just because. How could he possibly top that?

The phone rang yet again, cutting Angela's daydreams short.

"Where are you?" Marcus said as she picked up the phone. "I thought you'd be outside waiting."

"Hey sweetie, I'm sorry. You're here already?"

"Just come downstairs. I'm in the visitors' parking lot." Angela couldn't quite read his voice. He sounded so formal.

She didn't know if her sigh was audible as she thought about going straight sista girl on his behind. But remembering that there was probably a surprise awaiting her, she decided not to go off on him, and instead changed her tune abruptly.

"Give me five minutes," Angela said.

With the crazy way she'd been feeling, Angela could only imagine what she looked like as she exited the One-Ninety-One building on the world famous Peachtree Street. Once through the revolving doors, she paused momentarily to catch her breath as the Hotlanta August sun greeted her, then continued on through the circular driveway toward the visitors' parking lot. Her long, slightly bowlegged stride made her hips move in a way that only a sista could pull off; her honey brown eyes squinted slightly as she impatiently combed the busy lot for their black Expedition.

Finally spotting the truck, Angela slowly began to smile. Seeing Marcus immediately calmed the restless feeling that had been troubling her all day.

Angela hopped into the truck and gave Marcus a quick peck on the lips, then frowned a bit as she noticed how he was looking at her. His eyes seemed to be taking her in intently, from head to toe, as she settled into the passenger seat.

"Hey, sweetie. What's up?" She forced a smile to mask the flutters that had begun again in her stomach.

Something still didn't feel right, but Angela couldn't quite put her finger on it. As she sank back into the cool leather seat, she checked out her husband's profile. He wore a white dress shirt, topped off by a Brooks Brothers bowtie she'd bought him for Christmas the year before. At almost thirty-four, he looked like a big Hershey's kiss, with long eyelashes and pearly whites that other folks paid for. And since bald heads had come into style, his premature hair loss didn't even hurt him. In fact, the smooth head only added to his sex appeal.

On this day, Marcus looked as handsome as ever, but there was something that Angela still couldn't quite put her finger on. Since Marcus frequently accused her of overanalyzing, she tried to quiet her mind and instead figure out where her surprise was hiding.

"So . . . don't keep me guessing," she started. "Why'd you drag me out of work? Did you miss me too much to wait until I got home?" Angela raised her left eyebrow in a gesture of playfulness that was not returned.

"Angela, I need to ask you something, and I need for you to be completely honest with me," he said, without looking directly at her.

Still scanning the truck for evidence of her gift, Angela glanced at Marcus in hopes that he wouldn't notice he had only half of her attention.

"Ok. What's up? What do you want to know?"

"I need to know who you've been talking to," he said softly, staring at the steering wheel as if it held the answer to his question.

Angela started to laugh, wondering what kind of game he was playing. This was a new one. Did she have to play twenty questions to get her gift?

"What are you talking about?" she asked, rubbing his arm to thaw his cool disposition. Happy as Angela was to see him, and excited as she was about her surprise, he needed to speed this up if she was ever going to get out of work at a decent hour.

Marcus took in a deep breath, and eased his arm away from her. Clenching and unclenching his hands, he closed his eyes and appeared to calm himself. Then he placed his hands back on the steering wheel, and started again.

"Angela, I'm serious. I had lunch with Charles today, and he knew some things that only you and I know. Baby, I need for you to be honest with me."

Her heartbeat increased, just a tad. Had she been gossiping about something that Marcus found out about? Angela knew that Marcus didn't want a lot of people to know the details of his work situation, but figured that was just male pride and ego because business wasn't taking off as quickly as he wanted. She didn't think he'd mind her talking to the girls about his projects. And besides, Angela was pretty sure she hadn't told them anything he wouldn't have told them himself.

Still smiling, although a bit tentatively, Angela carefully asked, "Sweetie, what are you talking about? What kind of things did Charles know? Who would I be talking to?" She quickly glanced at the clock on the dash of the car, wondering if this was something they could finish up later. If she didn't get that memo done that night, she was going to get fired – plain and simple.

Clenching and unclenching his fists again, Marcus turned to look at her in full. That's when she first noticed that his eyes were a little red and sad-looking. He looked . . . different. In fact, as she looked closer, he appeared to be on the brink of tears, which was alarming, since crying didn't typically come easily for Marcus. He was one of those guys who thought real men should suck it up, and let it out only when they're about to explode.

"Angela, I need for you to tell me everything now. Maybe we can still work through this, but I can't do anything if I don't know who knows what. Charles was saying things to me that only you know, so I need to know who you've been talking to." His voice was barely above a whisper – so soft that Angela could hear the wind whistling outside her window as raindrops began to fall.

"Like Charles asked me if I'm having trouble sleeping," he continued. "It's like he knew about me waking up the past few nights. No one could know that but you and me."

Angela sat there quietly as she tried to figure out what in the world he could be talking about. *He's upset because his friend asked if he's been having problems sleeping?* This didn't make any sense.

"I need for you to tell me who you've been talking to!" he suddenly yelled.

Despite her best efforts to appear calm, Angela shivered involuntarily. Marcus sounded delusional, but that didn't make any sense so she couldn't allow her mind to dwell there. There had to be a logical explanation for what was happening.

"I don't know who's talking to who. I don't know who all is involved," he ranted, "but if I can just figure out who's behind this, I can beat it. The government? The Internet company? Enron? Who is it? Am I going to jail? Is that what this is about? What did they do to make you talk?" His words came out in a jumble without his stopping to come up for air, as she sat there in a daze.

"Of all the people involved, I just never suspected you," he said, finally looking at her directly. "Baby, just tell me who you talked to, and how they got to you. Please!" His eyes watered, and Angela looked away because she couldn't absorb any more.

She tried to quiet the growing fear inside of her. She told herself to stay calm, that everything would be okay, but her self wasn't quite buying it.

"Marcus, I don't know what you're talking about," Angela said in what she hoped to be a soothing voice. "I haven't talked to Charles or anyone else about your sleeping or anything. I honestly don't know what you're talking about. But you're starting to scare me."

Something in her words must have struck a chord inside of him, because Marcus began to sob. "Something's wrong with me. If I can't trust my wife, something must be wrong. . . I think I need to talk to someone."

Angela's heart raced through her throat as she finally fully realized that he was dead serious – that this was dead serious.

Something is wrong. Something is really wrong with Marcus. What are we going to do?

6

HIS FACE WAS A CONSORTIUM OF EMOTIONS, AS MARCUS seemed to fall apart before her eyes. Guilt, shame, fear, and anger took turns occupying the face that usually bore an armor of confidence.

"I just want to kill myself. That's what I'm going to do. Yeah, I'm going to kill myself," he said, while crying unabashedly.

Angela sat beside him in the parked car trying to figure out what to do. At a loss for words, she finally moved toward Marcus to hold him. But before she could get close, he halted her with his eyes. His eyes said that he didn't want her to touch him, didn't want her to see him in this state.

"Marcus, talk to me, sweetie. Tell me what's going on. I don't understand. . ." Angela grasped in vain for the words to make things right, but for once, she didn't have any.

"I tried to get in to talk to a counselor today. . . but I couldn't get an appointment," he said quickly, but then stopped abruptly when fresh tears began to fall.

"I don't know what's going on, baby, but we've got to get someone to help us fix it." Angela's voice was a mere whisper as a single tear slid down her cheek. "We're going to find someone to talk to tonight. We're going to find some way to make things ok again. . . Ok?"

When he didn't respond, Angela again moved to console him, but he turned toward the window as if he didn't want to be touched. Angela tried to put aside her hurt so she could think.

In the split second that followed, she decided that she'd have to find a counselor that he could see right away. Everything would be fine, if she could just find someone for him to talk to. All she needed to do is get her purse from upstairs, and stay cool.

Looking over at Marcus, Angela saw that her confident, manly husband was slumped over the steering wheel, trying to regain his composure. She unlocked her door and reached to open it, while trying to figure out how she could convince him to give her the keys from the ignition.

"Wait," he whined in an almost childlike voice. "You can't leave me here alone." He looked afraid for her to leave, as if she was the glue holding him together.

"What? . . . Marcus, I have to get my purse from upstairs so we can go find a doctor. . . I'll be right back." Angela's hands shook slightly as she wiped her eyes and moved again to get out of the car, still trying to figure out how to discreetly grab the keys.

"But who will you talk to upstairs? Are you going to call someone? Or is someone coming here for me?"

Angela tried not to panic at what Marcus was saying. It didn't make any sense. All she needed to do was get her purse and figure out where to go at this hour.

"I'm not staying here alone. . . . . I'm coming with you," he said, obviously deciding that trusting her was not an option.

Angela's face flushed as she paused with her hand on the door.

"Ok . . . uh . . . well, we'll just go right upstairs and we're not going to talk to anyone. . . Ok?" Angela peered into the truck's mirror and dabbed at her eyes again, as if she could magically wipe away the past fifteen minutes.

Minutes and hours seemed irrelevant, so Angela wasn't sure how long it took them to get up to her office. Angela jammed the button next to 36 a few times for good measure, as she wondered if the elevator was always so slow. She could feel Marcus' breath on the back of her neck, so she knew he was close, but she dared not turn around to face him. She didn't want to face him or the reality of what was happening.

Then she heard the voice again, only this time it said something new. *You've got to do this.*

By the time the elevator doors finally opened on her floor, Angela felt as if she might faint from unconsciously holding her breath for so long. Charging through the elevator doors, security pass in hand, she hoped that Marcus would follow quietly behind her. She acknowledged the few people that they passed in the building hallway, giving them a quick nod, and kept moving. What felt like hours later, they finally made it through the secured doors of the firm and on to her office. Fortunately, none of her colleagues had lingered or tried to make conversation, so the two of them were able to get there without any real interaction.

Angela quickly unlocked the bottom desk drawer and pulled out her briefcase, then absentmindedly shut down her computer as Marcus watched intently from the corner of her office.

Just when she thought they had made it undetected, Angela's secretary poked her head in the doorway. Even though they'd only been working together for a couple of months, Angela could tell that Trixie was a mother hen. Though she had to be nearly seventy years old, and probably only weighed a hundred pounds soaking wet, Angela had a feeling that Trixie was tougher than she looked.

"Angela," Trixie began, but then stopped mid-sentence when she noticed Marcus. "Oh, I'm sorry! I didn't realize you had someone in here with you." Trixie paused, obviously expecting Angela to introduce Marcus, but Angela said nothing. In fact, she didn't even make full eye contact – not even when she noticed Trixie glancing at the wedding photo on her bookshelf, probably to confirm that the man in her office was in fact Angela's husband. For once, Angela was glad to be the newbie at the firm. Made her feel a little more anonymous.

"Uh, well, I was just going to tell you that Nicole left some journal articles in your chair that she thought might be useful," she said.

"Thanks, Trixie. I'll see you tomorrow," Angela said, hoping that the words didn't sound as rude as she feared. Angela still dared not even look Trixie in the eye, as just one curious word or look could open the floodgates completely. She was immensely grateful that Trixie seemed to take the hint and left the office quickly.

Still trying to figure out their next move, Angela turned off the light, headed back through the halls of her firm, and down the elevator with Marcus in tow. The one time that Angela braved a glance back at him, he appeared to be in a daze. Gone was the dimpled smile that usually garnished his face, and in its place was the absence of any emotion.

When they reached the truck, Angela climbed into the driver's seat and was glad that Marcus quickly got into the car too. Without further delay, she started the Expedition and began driving down Peachtree Street. Before she'd even made it to the freeway, the dark sky opened and commenced to release a torrent of tears, as thunder rumbled in the distance.

Angela didn't know where they were going. She just hoped that it would all be better soon.

7

"WHOAH, THAT MIGHT HAVE BEEN ENOUGH TO make me run screaming from the car!" Mary says, more animated than I have seen her. "What were you thinking as you and Marcus were driving from your job?"

"I don't know," I respond. "I don't think there was time to think about anything."

"Are you sure?" Mary asks, tilting her head to the side with a small smile.

I sit there trying to take myself back to that awful day. I see the truck parked at the curb. Remember my excitement as I open the door; then my confusion as I see his face. Feel the flutter of my heart as I try not to panic when his words don't make sense.

"I don't know what I was thinking," I finally say, "so much as what I was trying not to think."

"Okay, let's go with that. What were you suppressing?"

A beat passes as I struggle to dig up memories planted someplace I'd hoped not to go again.

"All I remember is that I kept telling myself that everything was ok and that nothing was wrong. That he'd be okay. That we'd be okay."

"What else Angela?" Mary's voice is kind, but strong, so I know there is no wiggling my way out of this one.

"I don't know."

"Take a minute and just tell me whatever comes to mind."

I see my hand on the car door, and feel my excitement as I wonder what Marcus has planned for me, then confusion as I realize nothing is as it should be. I feel myself falling, then my resolve to find a way to make things right again.

"I guess –" I start, then pause as I see myself back in the car hoping that none of it is real. "Somehow, if I didn't admit that something was wrong, it didn't seem so bad. Guess I kind of checked out. If I'd stopped to think about whether he was going to be okay, or about the fact that my period hadn't started, or any of those things to make it real, I wouldn't have made it."

"Okay. Have you done this before?"

"Definitely."

"Like when?"

"Like when my father died," I say, marveling that for some reason a 10 year-old memory brings tears back to my eyes.

"Ok. Help me understand how you process. When bad things happen, what do you do?"

Who has time to process, I want to ask, but don't. Instead, I see the confusion on Marcus' face and hear myself telling him that I'm going up to get my purse. I sound so confident that I almost believe myself when I tell him we're going to find a way to make things right.

"It's like stepping outside my body, and watching from afar," I finally say. "Then I'm able to see how to stay in control. How to act the way I'm supposed to act, instead of really losing it. Then I can try to fix it."

Mary makes another quick note on her pad.

"That's definitely a common coping mechanism," she finally says. "And, it often gets us through a crisis. But, at some point in time, we have to step back in. We've got to allow ourselves to really process, and sometimes that means recognizing that we might not be able to fix everything.

"Know what I mean, Angela?"

8

SOMEWHERE IN THE DISTANCE A DJ ON THE RADIO was announcing an upcoming concert by Angela's favorite Atlanta artist, while the man next to her cried shamelessly about wanting to end his life. Angela tuned them both out, and silently prayed that they would get to the hospital quickly.

It was like watching television on mute. She distanced herself from the scene playing out in front of her, because if she didn't, they'd never make it. Her continuous prayers were like a tourniquet that kept the wound from bleeding out, and if she stopped – even for just a moment to acknowledge that the shell of a man crying next to her was Marcus – she knew she'd fall apart.

Angela had been that way since she was a little girl. The one who calmly called 911 when her little cousin busted his head open as he ran into the glass edge of a dining room table. The one who waited until after her father's death, funeral arrangements, and post-death responsibilities to really cry. She wasn't sure if it was adrenaline from the crisis, or fear of losing it completely, that pushed her into auto-pilot mode. But that was how she always made it through.

Somewhere between the parking lot and freeway, Angela had decided to take Marcus to a psychiatric facility in southwest Atlanta. She'd never had any firsthand experience with the hospital, but knew from commercials that they dealt with emotional issues. Now that it was after normal business hours, their options were limited, and this was clearly something that couldn't wait until morning. Marcus had been crying since they got into the truck. It was as if someone had flipped a switch to "on," and he'd suddenly swung to the other end of the spectrum from his normal composed self. Once they turned out of the parking lot of her office he had begun to sob hysterically. Angela focused on trying to take in full and even breaths, though it felt like a shortage of oxygen in the car.

"I should just kill myself! That's what I should do. I should just jump out of the car!" Marcus had exclaimed, seemingly from out of nowhere. That was the last thing Angela heard before she turned down the volume and tuned inward to prayer.

It was the longest drive of her life.

Forty-five minutes through stop-and-go traffic during one of Atlanta's infamous thunderstorms. The downtown skyline was but a blur as she wove in and out between cars, trying to move more quickly. Angela counted exits as she drove south on the connector in an attempt to distract herself from what was going on around her. There were four exits before she reached I-20, where she merged onto the expressway heading west. Thankfully there was far less congestion on I-20 and she moved quickly past the Atlanta University Center, then on through the West End. In an effort to stay calm she again began counting exits. Six before she reached I-285. Only a few more to their destination.

Marcus' crying grew softer and seemed to blend in with crooning from the radio. Both were background to the sound of Angela's beating heart, which sounded like a bass line in one of T.I.'s tracks and felt as if it might burst through her chest at any moment.

She reached the Camp Creek exit and turned in the opposite direction from the airport. It should be close.

Angela drove past the new shopping center and other residential developments before finally spotting signs for Peachtree Hospital on her right. She parked in a handicapped spot in front and turned off the ignition. Only then did she dare look at Marcus.

His arms were crossed in front of him, his forehead pressed against the passenger windowpane. He rocked back and forth slowly, as if moving to a beat that only he could hear.

"Marcus?" Angela touched his arm tentatively. "Sweetie, we need to get out now."

He hesitated long enough for Angela to wonder if he'd heard her, then as if pulling out of a trance, finally turned in her direction. The heaviness in his eyes crushed something inside of her.

They stared at each other momentarily. Angela looked away first.

Without further discussion, he opened the car door and got out, then walked up the sidewalk with Angela following closely behind. They walked into the hospital together – Angela and the broken man who had taken the place of her husband.

She braced herself for the mixture of smells that she associated with hospitals and sick people, and for the sight of crazy folks in straitjackets, banging their heads against the walls like she'd seen in the movies. But when they walked into the office area, Angela breathed a sigh of relief as she inhaled the calming scent of lavender, and saw only a handful of very normal-looking people sitting quietly. Bland wood tables provided space for the popular magazines that must be standard fare for offices, and the too-white walls were clean and bare. It looked like any other doctor's office.

She quickly strode over to the petite blond sitting at the reception desk, while Marcus paced the floor in the space beside her.

"We . . . um . . . my husband needs to talk to someone." Angela hoped the receptionist heard her mumbled words. And even more, she hoped the counselor would understand without the need for details. How do you explain that everything was beautifully normal, but then something snapped and now it's not normal anymore?

"Of course. You've come to the right place. I can get one of our counselors for you, if you'd like to have a seat."

"Will it take long?" Angela asked, then added in an even lower tone, "He says he wants to kill himself."

"I'll get someone right away." The receptionist immediately picked up the phone, but her expression remained inscrutable. Angela couldn't hear what was said, but within a few minutes the door beside the receptionist magically opened and a woman beckoned them inside.

"Hi, I'm Vicki," the counselor began with a reassuring smile, as the door closed behind them. She looked and spoke directly to Marcus, but simultaneously placed a hand on Angela's shoulder as if to say "It's going to be ok."

"We're just going to find a quiet room and talk a little bit about what brings you here today," she explained, after Marcus and Angela had introduced themselves.

Vicki led Marcus down the sterile, empty hallway, with Angela trailing in the rear. By then, he had stopped crying and instead was looking like his mind was somewhere else. Unlike his normal Denzel stroll, Marcus walked with his head slightly bowed and his shoulders drooped. Angela couldn't bear to look at his fragile demeanor, so she turned her attention instead to Vicki.

Vicki was a rather plain-looking woman, with only a pair of small pearl earrings as adornment. Her khaki pants appeared to be at least a size too small and did nothing to flatter what Angela guessed to be a size 16 sista-girl behind. Her hair looked like she'd stuck one roller above her forehead before bed, and left the rest to chance. But when Vicki smiled, her face glowed in a way that portrayed beauty and warmth from within. Her smile instantly made Angela feel that this place just might be ok. Angela tried to hold on to that positive energy.

Soon they were seated in a room that was only slightly bigger than Angela's walk-in closet at home. Suddenly the house, car, and all the material items they possessed seemed trite. She would give it all up without a second thought if it would get them through this.

Vicki handed her some forms to fill out and then began talking to Marcus in a soft voice. "So . . . what brings you here today?"

Marcus looked at Angela, then back to Vicki without responding. He appeared to be trying to show his normal machismo, but then stopped short of pulling it off.

"I keep having these thoughts that I can't get rid of," he began haltingly. "I guess it goes back to when I quit my job as a consultant and started my own business. First, I partnered with this guy named Lee, and he turned out to be kind of shady. So I stopped doing business with him, and he started telling folks bad things about me and my company. . . ."

That part was true. Angela hadn't liked Lee from the first time they met. That's also around the time Marcus stopped sleeping, consumed with what people might think of the things Lee might be saying. *He'd just been stressed; that's all, right?*

"And I was getting all these letters and calls from the consulting company about the signing bonus they'd given me . . . saying they wanted it back since I stayed there less than a year. . . ."

She had almost forgotten about that. Definitely another reason he'd been worried. Maybe he just needed to talk it out. Maybe Angela should have realized how much this was bothering him.

"And then . . .well, weird things started happening, like my friend, Charles, was asking questions about my business and things about me that only my wife would know. . . ." He paused and glanced briefly at Angela.

"I don't know. I know it sounds crazy, even to me. . . but it just seemed . . . like . . . everybody . . . was against me or something." Marcus' soliloquy ended with a slight chuckle, as if he knew how absurd he sounded.

"Marcus, it's ok to tell me what's going on," Vicki began. "Think of it this way. The mind is just like any other part of the body. When you run it into the ground, sometimes it needs a break. If you won't take one, it takes one on its own. So it's ok if you had weird thoughts about things going on. Really, it's going to be fine."

Angela didn't know if Marcus felt better after hearing Vicki's explanation, but Angela felt as if she'd exhaled for the first time in at least two hours. Vicki had to be right. In the eleven years that Angela had known Marcus, he'd been a rock. He was the "big man on campus" in undergrad, a well-traveled officer in the Air Force, the holder of a graduate degree, and was on his way to building the business he'd always dreamed of. He couldn't be normal one minute and crack up completely in the next. Could he?

Without saying more to Vicki, Marcus kept looking up to make sure Angela was ok. Even in his impaired state, he was trying to take care of her. He squared his shoulders and quickly wiped his eye with the back of his hand.

Vicki must have sensed Marcus' preoccupation because she turned to face Angela. "I'm sure the two of you haven't eaten anything and it's after seven. Why don't you go get something to eat, Angela, and give Marcus and me a chance to talk a little more?"

Angela felt torn. On one hand, this was her husband and he needed her now more than ever. On the other hand, he obviously didn't want her to see him like this. Heck, she didn't want to see him like this either. She just wanted to rewind the clock and make everything ok again.

"Marcus, what do you want me to do?"

He refused to return Angela's gaze directly, answering her question without saying a word.

Angela felt more alone than ever before, but she knew it would only make matters worse if she broke down now. Somebody had to be the strong one.

"Ok . . . well, um . . . I'll be back soon. . . I have my cell if you need me, sweetie."

And with that, she was gone.

Black folks and food. Be it a wedding, funeral, family drama, or mental issue, food is the end-all, be-all. Angela always assumed it was because food soothed the soul. But now she realized that food keeps the mind occupied so that you don't have to think about whatever craziness you have going on. Heading out to get food now gave her a purpose, and it helped her think about something other than the fact that her husband's mind had fallen apart.

Her stomach growled loudly, forcing her to remember how long it had been since she last ate. She knew she needed to take care of herself, especially if she were pregnant. But she couldn't process that now.

Angela climbed into the car, then decided she needed to call someone for support. Her first thought was to call her good friend, Naomi. After all, she was a psychologist. But, thinking on it more, she realized that was precisely why she couldn't call Naomi. She would try to play doctor and Angela wasn't ready for that.

There was only one person who would understand: Endia. Unfortunately, Endia knew first-hand about mental issues because her little sister was bipolar. Angela could still remember how hard it was when Endia's sister had experienced her first episode and was hospitalized. Wendy had disappeared for a full day before finally being picked up by the police for driving recklessly. Apparently, she'd been swerving to avoid hitting things in the road that only she could see. Thank God Angela didn't have to deal with something permanent like that.

She picked up her cell phone and hit "2," then waited for an answer. The phone rang several times, then went to voicemail.

Angela said a silent prayer that her friend would pick up on the vibe that she was needed. Desperately. Then, she hit "2" and waited again.

An older white man peered into Angela's car as he walked past in the parking lot. His gait was confident and measured, like that of a soldier, but his eyes personified what Angela felt: fear that the very thing that mattered most might be lost. She closed her eyes and prayed as the phone rang again.

"Hello?" Endia sounded breathless, as if she may have run to the phone. Angela could just picture Endia, with her normal cut-to-the-chase attitude, impatiently tapping her foot at the silence she got in response to the greeting.

"Hello-o-o?" Endia said again, this time with less friendliness. Knowing her friend, Angela knew that Endia was about three seconds away from hanging up the phone.

Angela wanted to speak, but nothing was coming out. Her mouth moved, and her brain was struggling to form coherent sentences, but she could not utter a single sound. It was as if putting the day's events into words made it real, and the fear became paralyzing. A sob broke before she could say anything intelligible.

"Who is this?" Endia asked, the alarm seeming to rise in her voice. "Who's there?" Angela had forgotten that her friend didn't have caller ID on her home phone. Strangely enough, however, Endia didn't sound like she thought it was a prank or a wrong number.

"It's Angie," she finally managed to whisper. "I'm at Peachtree Hospital with Marcus," she added, then began to sob uncontrollably. For the first time since the entire ordeal started, Angela let the reality of the situation set in.

"Oh my God!" Endia said. "What happened?"

Angela quickly summarized the events of the day, through intermittent sobs and gasps for air, and wondered if Endia could even follow her rambling tale.

"Have they told you anything? What are they saying?" Endia asked.

"No, I haven't really talked to anyone yet. . . All I know is that he's talking to a counselor now. The counselor said he was probably just stressed and –" The fear rose from the pit of her stomach to her throat and back down again.

"Angie, do you want me to come there? It's too late for me to catch a flight tonight, but I'm sure I can find one early tomorrow."

Angela opened her mouth to say no. After all, she was the independent one who prided herself on being super strong. She was the counselor and mediator amongst her friends, rarely leaving room for them to return the favor. She never needed help . . . until now.

"What about your job? You can't just take time from the agency like this. Did you even finish shooting your commercial? And a flight from Chicago to Atlanta at the last minute would cost a fortune," Angela said weakly.

Endia had known Angela for almost twelve years, so she had to know that anything short of a "no, of course not" meant that Angela was hurting pretty badly. This was as close as Angela could come to saying, "I can't do this without you."

"You let me worry about all that. I'm going to call now to check on flights. I'll call you back to let you know what time I get in . . . Ok?"

Angela couldn't say anything.

"Ok?"

"Ok," she finally replied. "And one more thing . . . Could you please call Christine too? I just . . . I just can't."

"Of course, babygirl, I'll call her now. What about Naomi? Maybe she can come and sit with you tonight?"

"Nah, I'm not ready to talk to anyone here just yet."

"Ok, I understand. Just didn't want you to be alone. I'll call you later. Ok?"

Down again went the floodgate of tears. This time she didn't attempt to hold them back, though she knew she was creating quite a show for folks who passed by in the parking lot. Each one looked in, then quickly away – likely because they didn't want to be involved. Or, maybe the weight of their own grief and fears was all they could bear.

I'm not alone, Angela told herself. She wanted to tell Endia to hurry to Atlanta. Angela wanted to ask if Endia could come that night, and wanted to tell her how much she didn't want to be by herself for another minute. But instead, she simply said ok and hung up the phone.

She spent the next half hour driving around, trying to figure out what kind of food to get. It's like her brain had stopped functioning and made the most simple decisions overwhelming. Whole chicken or nuggets? Original or crispy? Anything to keep from asking the overriding question beneath the surface: *What happens now?*

By the time she returned to the hospital, Angela was no closer to winning the battle with her fear. *He's going to be ok.* That's the mantra she repeated to herself as she reentered the room where Marcus and Vicki still sat talking. Both of them silently acknowledged her presence with a nod, but neither broke stride when she came through the door.

"Marcus, what do you think about staying here overnight?" Vicki asked. "Maybe talking to one of our doctors tomorrow morning about some of the thoughts you've been having? I really think they can help."

Angela could just imagine what he must be thinking: "Marcus Bennett, spend the night in a mental hospital? Heck no! Out of the question. I'm not crazy, so why should I stay at a crazy hospital?" She tried to force a reassuring smile to let Marcus know that she supported him in whatever decision he made, but she was sure that her smile did nothing to mask the red rim of her eyes and the fatigue in her normally high-energy stance.

"I want to do whatever needs to be done to get through this," he started, sounding as authoritative as his normal self. "Angie, what do you think I should do?"

Angela blinked back tears, and paused momentarily to consider their options. She almost chuckled at the irony of a woman who couldn't even decide on dinner, making a decision about her husband's stay in a mental hospital. How could she take home a man who couldn't trust her? Her mind flashed back to the wild-eyed accusations Marcus had made in the car. She remembered the redness in his eyes, his clenched fists, and the way he yelled. This man was a stranger. As much as she wanted to, she couldn't take him home.

"I think it's a good idea to stay here, sweetie. Maybe they can help," she said, struggling to give him a reassuring smile.

Marcus looked at her intently, as if trying to decipher any hidden motives. Then his face softened. "I trust you. I know you want what's best for me, so if you think I should stay, then that's what I'll do."

Vicki handed Marcus some papers, which he signed without hesitation. Once the paperwork was taken care of, the counselor led them out of the room and back down one of the halls through which they had entered. They walked down the hallway with as much enthusiasm as those in a funeral line, waiting to say their final goodbyes. Angela wrinkled her nose as a somewhat familiar smell greeted her. Not antiseptic and death as she remembered. This time it was antiseptic and fear. As if someone had tried to wash away the bad, but only succeeded in making it worse.

The three of them walked past a doorway and turned in the direction of the reception desk. Continuing down this empty corridor, they eventually came to a second door. Pausing momentarily, Vicki pushed the buzzer and some invisible force opened it from within. Vicki stepped through the doorway and motioned for Marcus to follow.

"You'll need to say good-bye here," Vicki told them.

The surprise on Marcus' face matched what Angela was feeling. Suddenly it seemed all wrong, and Angela felt like maybe this wasn't such a good idea after all. But what other choice did they have?

"Angie, I think I should go home. I don't think you should leave me here." His eyes begged her to understand and to help. "I've changed my mind."

Tears began to fill Angela's eyes as a feeling of helplessness overtook her.

"I mean, why would I be staying here anyway? For a bunch of so-called doctors to run game on me, and who think I'm crazy?" Marcus said, in his normal take charge tone.

Angela looked down at the ground in hopes that it would swallow her up before she caved in and took her man home. Obviously sensing Angela's weakness, Vicki pulled Marcus gently but firmly inside.

"Please, Angie, I want to go home," he said, in a voice that sounded young and scared.

Before Angela had time to fully process what was happening, the doors shut and locked behind them. Leaving her husband on one side, and Angela on the other.

9

NGELA TURNED THE KEY AND OPENED THE FRONT door to their home, then exhaled deeply at the silence that greeted her. She took in the large ebony entertainment center and cream leather sofas in their family room, and everything else that was just as they'd left it that morning. Her "getting ready for work" routine that day felt like it had occurred years earlier. The corner of her eye pulled in their wedding photo, prominently displayed over the fireplace, and it was hard to remember how the smiling faces in the photo had comforted her only hours before.

Angela couldn't believe that she'd just left her husband at a mental hospital. Why didn't she notice that something was bothering him? She searched her mind for clues she'd missed, pulling up only fragments. His sleepless nights. His unending questions over what people might be thinking about the fact that his business had yet to take off. Even his recent statements about feeling unsupported could have been linked to this.

Things that had seemed so normal only days before now caused Angela to question. Had she missed something?

After changing into some boxer shorts and one of Marcus' white t-shirts, Angela felt her stomach growl. This reminded her that it had been at least nine hours since she'd eaten; the food she purchased during the trip out of the hospital had gone untouched.

Angela walked slowly into the kitchen and opened the pantry to see what she could pull together. She knew that she didn't have the mental or physical energy to cook anything, so she grabbed a box of cereal from the pantry and a gallon of milk from the refrigerator. The stainless-steel door was littered with magnets from all the places they'd visited. Puerto Rico, where they'd taken a military hop for an inexpensive honeymoon. Sicily, where she'd visited Marcus while he was on a Mediterranean tour. Cancun, where they'd watched the sunset and talked about how many more sunsets they'd see in the seventy years they planned to spend together.

Balancing a bowl and spoon in one hand, cereal under her arm, and milk in the other hand, she mindlessly went to the breakfast table and sat down.

Though she'd done it many times before, sitting alone in the empty house right now felt foreign.

As she poured her cereal and then the milk, Angela's mind kept churning. She wondered how long he'd been stressed and why she didn't see it. Finally, she promised to stop beating up on herself.

Angela picked up the phone, pressed "1," and hit "talk. Then, thinking better of it, she quickly pressed "end" and put the phone back down on the table as if it were a hot potato.

Several minutes passed as Angela sat there, staring at the phone while silently praying that it wouldn't ring. The idea of talking to her mother usually comforted her, but now all she felt was tired. If she told her mom what was going on, she'd want to hop on a plane from Florida to come visit. Plus, she'd want to talk about how she tried to warn Angela a few weeks before, and Angela didn't want to hear it. Not to mention that she'd tell the rest of the family, and Marcus would forever be stigmatized as the one who was in the crazy hospital.

Thankful that she'd made the right decision and confident that the call to her mom must not have gone through, she picked up the phone again. This time Angela dialed Endia, hoping she wasn't already sleeping. Fortunately, Endia picked up on the first ring.

"Hey, chica, I'm glad to hear from you. I was about to call you with our flight information."

Angela felt her eyes brim with tears. "You mean, you're really coming? And Christine too?"

"Of course, we're really coming. I told you I was checking on flights. Christine and I were even able to get on the same flight tomorrow. We fly in on Delta arriving at 11:15 a.m."

Tears streamed down Angela's face as she realized how much she didn't want to be alone. Her girls were coming to take care of her, and she was going to let them, instead of playing her usual role as the strong one. She was not alone.

"Angie? Are you there?"

"Yeah," she whispered, "I'm just really glad you're coming. I don't know what to say. I feel like such a baby for having you and Chris fly all the way down here just to hold my hand."

"Boy, you really suck at this," Endia said, chuckling softly. "So here's how it goes. When friends do things for their friends, the person on the receiving end says 'thank you.' That's it. Nothing more. Got it?"

Angela smiled wanly, then after a slight pause responded, "But you know how . . . "

"What?"

"My bad . . . um . . . Thank you."

"Enough on that. Have you talked to Marcus' family?"

"Nah, I haven't called them yet. I figure it's no use worrying them tonight before we know what's going on. It's not like he's that close to them anyway. I'm going to wait until after we talk to the doctors then see what he wants to tell them.

"But I know he's going to be ok. I was freaking out earlier, but now I'm believing and expecting a good report from the doctors. Marcus just needs some rest. He's been going at it pretty hard trying to get his business up and running, ya know? Not getting much sleep and just stressed about making this work. . . I shouldn't have pushed him so hard."

There was a brief pause on the line before Endia responded. Angela was beginning to think they'd gotten disconnected when Endia finally spoke up. "Well, we're praying . . . And you can't blame yourself. You didn't do anything wrong. Now let's talk about you. Have you called your mom yet? I'm sure you'll feel better when you talk to her."

"Nah, not yet. I know she and the rest of my family would want to help . . . I just don't want to worry them until I know what's what. I wouldn't even know what to say now." Angela tried to rub the tension out of her neck, as she envisioned having to make that call.

"Well, when you're ready, you should call them. And you should call Naomi too. Your family and friends would want to be there for you."

"I know. It's just that some people hear 'mental hospital' and immediately think of worst-case scenarios. I don't want Marcus to have to deal with that when this is over. Not even with family."

Another long pause in response. Not knowing what to make of it, Angela asked, "Endia, what are you doing?"

"Huh? I'm here . . . Look, we'll be there not long after you wake up. Do we need to take a cab, or maybe we should take the MARTA to a stop close to your house? That might make it easier on you."

"Oh no, girl, I'll pick you two up from the airport. I'm not going to work tomorrow, and from what the hospital told me, I can't see Marcus until Saturday. I'm going to go nuts if I just sit here. Picking you up will at least give me something to do."

"Cool."

"Also, when you talk back to Chris, will you tell her that I'll just talk to her when she gets here? I'm really glad she's coming, but I just don't feel like going through the story of what happened again, so I haven't returned her calls . . . I called you 'cause I knew you'd understand."

"Girl, please. I'm sure she's not trippin' on a return call right now. Besides, we'll be there in person soon enough."

"Yeah . . . Anyway, Endi, I know you probably need to pack and stuff."

"Yeah, I do. But you call me if you need me, ok? Doesn't matter what time . . ."

"Thanks, girl," Angela said.

"Love you."

"Love you too."

Her now soggy cereal no longer looked appealing. Since she didn't have an appetite anyway, she dumped it down the garbage disposal and went to get into bed. The clock on the nightstand read 11:15, but Angela wasn't the least bit sleepy.

She lay in bed, staring up at the ceiling, with the covers pulled up under her chin, and tried unsuccessfully to will her mind to give it a rest. *A person can't just turn crazy overnight, can they? Could this be what Mom dreamed about? No way.* Angela shook her head as if to physically clear the negative thoughts and energy.

The king-sized pillow pressing against her body did little to assuage the loneliness, even when she pretended that Marcus was coming to bed soon. Instead, his empty side of the bed underscored her emotional void and made her mind race with still more questions. Angela closed her eyes and said another prayer, then rubbed her stomach and prayed again for their future.

The clock on the nightstand read 11:16.

Angela closed her eyes and did one of the insomnia exercises she still remembered from childhood. Beginning with her feet, she tensed each muscle, then relaxed. Ankles. Calves. Thighs.

The clock on the nightstand read 11:20.

In an attempt to relax, she pulled the pillow in more closely, shut her eyes, and inhaled Marcus: Lever soap, a hint of slightly sweet cologne, and the natural essence of him.

Kissing him goodnight in her dreams, Angela promised that she wouldn't let go.

10

I T WAS FRIDAY MORNING, AND ALMOST TIME FOR HER
alarm clock to go off. That would be when she'd normally
begin pressing snooze and begging God to magically dispense
with her need to work for a living. She'd press snooze at least
once more before Marcus finally turned off the clock, then
pulled her close, kissed the back of her neck and whispered in
her ear.

"Baby, it's time to get up."

Angela smiled at the sound of his voice, the familiarity of
his touch. Without opening her eyes, she reached a hand out
instinctively to her right. The cold mattress beside her was
initially a surprise, as the events of the night before surfaced
in her mind. Her fingers quickly withdrew from the emptiness
where her husband should have been.

Though she was accustomed to Marcus keeping late hours,
she'd never gotten used to sleeping alone. Instead, she'd drift in
and out of fitful dreams, waiting for the sound of him climbing
into bed. The crisp air would greet her as he pulled the covers
back to get in. Even before he touched her, she'd sense his energy
coming closer until their arms and legs were entangled, and they
each found their comfort zone. He'd give her a kiss goodnight
and then she'd finally feel herself floating away. With any luck,
she'd doze off before his loud snores ruined any chance of sleep.
I'd give anything to have some snoring to complain about now.

The night before had been a radical departure from her usual sleep routine. Angela had found herself lying in their bed with her eyes wide open. No matter how hard she tried to rest, she'd spent the night floating in and out of strange dreams. She started to get up to drink a glass – or hell, bottle – of wine to help her sleep. But she didn't like to drink alone and upset, and she didn't need to drink if she was preg . . .

Shaking her head at questions she wasn't ready to consider, Angela held a picture of Marcus in her mind as she'd seen him in her dream the night before. He was dressed in a dark suit, standing at a podium, as if preparing to give a speech. The crowd sat poised, ready for him to begin. He stood there smiling for several minutes, then opened his mouth to begin. But instead of speaking, he started to cry. He scanned the audience and finally found Angela in the front row, then cried even harder. "I'm so sorry," he said, over and over again. The dream left her disturbed, and still feeling guilty for not realizing before that her man was hurting. How long had he been suffering? How long had he been holding in his fears and stress?

Eleven years. Eleven years was a long time to know and love someone. Yet somehow she'd missed that something was seriously wrong. The only thing she could do now was love him through his healing. They'd move beyond this and everything would be ok. It just had to be.

Angela longed to put a pillow over her head and pretend that none of it was real, but the sound of the alarm interrupted Angela's thoughts and reminded her that the day was breaking. Before putting it off any longer, Angela picked up the phone and called to leave a voicemail for her secretary.

"Trixie, it's Angela." She paused to pull her thoughts together. "I've had a family emergency and I'm going to be out for a few days. You have my cell phone number if you need me."

Angela hoped that the nonspecific message would buy her some time while she figured out her story. In the meantime, she left a similar message for the partner with whom she was working most closely, along with a profuse apology and details on where to find the research she'd gathered for the memo. Thank goodness she hadn't been at the firm long enough to have any clients calling her directly. With any luck, the partners wouldn't write her off as some sort of flake, and would cover for her.

Angela looked at the clock and realized that it was almost 9:00 a.m. She would have stayed in bed all day if she didn't have to meet Endia and Christine at the airport. Since it was about a 45-minute drive and she still had to get ready, Angela was already behind schedule if she was to be on time to meet their 11:15 flight.

Entering the bathroom, Angela caught a glimpse of herself in the mirror. Wow. There was no way to hide how difficult the past seventeen hours had been. Her eyes were red and puffy from crying and lack of sleep, and her skin looked ashen. Who knew she could look pale? Even her hair was rebelling. Since she hadn't wrapped it the night before, every strand seemed to be going in its own direction.

Why bother? Angela thought as she abandoned any attempt to do her makeup or hair. She then struggled to pull on some jeans that were a tad snug, and a dark blue Howard University sweatshirt. Flip-flops and a navy bandana on her head made the outfit complete – completely hideous, that is. Angela normally wouldn't have been caught dead looking so bummed out, but today she just didn't care.

As if on auto-pilot, Angela made the drive to the airport and entered the passenger loading area. As always, there was a line of cars waiting to get to the interior curb to pick up loved ones.

Angela inched her way down to the very last door, marked N5, and finally managed to maneuver her way through the traffic to the curb. She sat there with her foot tapping impatiently, and the engine running, hoping her friends would hurry out before security forced her to circle around the airport again.

No more than five minutes later, Angela spotted her girls coming through the door. In typical fashion, Endia led the way to the airport exit with that take-no-prisoners walk of hers, followed closely by Christine. When Angela saw them headed for her car, the waterworks started again. The thought of her girls jumping on a plane to support her was almost too much. Angela considered again how she was generally the strong one who didn't need any help, and yet here she was needing them more than ever.

Endia wasted no time in hopping into the front passenger seat, and pulling Angela into a heartfelt embrace. "Hey, babygirl," she cooed, while rubbing Angela's back in a way that conveyed "You're not alone."

Endia had the biggest energy Angela had ever known. At only five feet five inches tall, with a small frame created by a life full of Pilates and veggies, you wouldn't think she would be as powerful. Instead, you might just size her up as being simply kind of different, what with her Badu-like bald head, chocolate skin, and unique fashion sense. Until you felt her energy. And at that moment, Angela had never been so grateful for it. For just a few seconds, she relaxed and felt better about everything.

The sound of Christine clearing her throat brought that moment to an end, and almost made Angela snicker. It had been the same since they'd all met in college. Christine never wanted to be left out, and that was probably magnified tenfold since Angela was the glue that bonded the other two friends.

In typical fashion, Christine now stood at the driver's door with one hand on her rolling bag and the other on her hip. "Hey there, missy," Christine said with a radiant smile, while bending down into the driver's window opening to kiss Angela's cheek.

If Endia were fire and energy, Christine was water and peace. She was a classic beauty, with stunning eyes and a smile that rivaled Diana Ross'. The only wild card was her hair, which she'd been trying to grow out naturally. Angela didn't think there was anything natural about struggling to get a comb through your hair, but they had agreed to disagree. Christine had the gift of bringing comfort where it was needed, and it sure was needed here.

Now that they had arrived, Angela felt suddenly unsure about what to do next. The hospital had told her that she couldn't see Marcus until the next day. So, until then, all she could do was wait and pray. She wouldn't even get an assessment from the doctors until then.

"Anybody else hungry?" Christine asked as she hopped into the back seat, grinning as if they were just hanging out during a normal girls' weekend. Classic Christine move to break the ice, and to be thinking about food. Made you wonder where she stored it all in that slender five-foot-seven-inch frame. But it worked. With little more discussion, they were off to an Indian restaurant that had become part of the routine during their previous visits to Atlanta.

The aroma of chicken tekka maki and saag paneer reminded Angela that it had been more than twenty-four hours since she'd eaten. She glanced around the table at her friends and felt so incredibly blessed.

"I'm so glad you guys are here!" Angela said, smiling in full for the first time in what seemed like forever.

"Girl, you need to stop. How could we not come?" Endia asked, while helping herself to a large piece of naan, the Indian bread that she swore had a trace of crack in it.

"You act as if you haven't been there for us over the years," Christine said. "You would have hopped on a plane just as quick for either one of us, and you know it.

"Remember when my parents got divorced and you just showed up, like it was nothing? Or what about when Endi's sister got sick? Plus, you know we love Marcus too. So you need to stop already."

"I hear ya," Angela said with a half-smile. It was true that the three of them had been through many an ordeal together.

"So, how are you really doing, babygirl?" Endia asked.

"I don't know," Angela said, answering truthfully. "I just can't believe any of this is happening. It doesn't even feel real."

"Yeah, I get that.

"I know the answer to this already, but is there anything we can do?"

Angela shook her head and said, "you've already done it. Just being here." She tried not to cry, but couldn't help it.

Christine and Endia's eyes watered, just seeing Angela's pain.

"Actually, there is one more thing you can do," Angela said.

"What?" they asked in unison.

"Can you just talk about something normal? Anything. For the next hour, I don't want to be the girl who left her husband at the hospital. I just want to pretend for a minute."

Her girlfriends both nodded, but said nothing.

"Seriously," Angela said. "Just talk. Please?"

"Well," Endia started hesitantly, "did Christine tell you she ran into Scott the other day?"

"You ran into Scott?" Angela asked, happy for something else to focus on. "The one and only 'I just love the way he says my name' – that Scott? When was this?"

"Ugh! Of all things, that's what you want to talk about?" Christine said, scowling at Endia.

Angela sat back and listened to the banter of her friends. Honestly she didn't catch everything they said, but just the joyful tone was enough to give her energy. In fact, it was so normal that Christine and Endia were soon bickering in a way that was common. Something about how Christine was always dating but repeatedly picking unavailable guys, and then a retort from Christine about how she'd at least had a date this decade. This was about to get ugly.

"Whoah, I know I said normal, but . . ." Angela said, then broke into a small giggle. Christine and Endia joined in laughing.

"It's good to see you smiling, Angie."

Angela had finally tucked the prior night's events into a hidden recess of her mind when her cell phone rang.

"Hold on," she said to her friends while pressing talk on her phone, noting the hospital's name and number on her caller ID.

"Hello?"

"Angela, you've got to come get me right now." Marcus sounded pathetic as he whispered into the phone.

Angela was thrown by the sound of utter panic in his voice, but she tried to remain calm. "What's wrong, sweetie? Is everything ok?"

"No, they're trying to kill me."

"What? Baby, what's happening? What do you mean?"

"Angela, listen to me. They – Are – Trying – To – Kill – Me! You've got to believe me and you've got to come and get me!" he whispered emphatically. Angela wondered how it was possible that he could sound worse than the night before when she left him. Was someone harming him? Should she have let him stay? But what other options did they have? Angela gripped the edge of the table to steady herself and willed her heartbeat to slow.

"Marcus, did something happen? What's going on?"

"Angela, they're definitely coming after me. They're all in on it. Maybe agents from the government – I haven't figured it all out yet – but I need to go home *now*."

Angela's stomach cramped at the realization that it was all in his head. Just like the evening before, only worse.

"Marcus, listen to me, sweetie. No one is going to hurt you, I promise. You need to stay there and talk to the doctors so you can work through this. Then it will all be better. Ok?"

Marcus said ok, but sounded like he'd just lost his best friend – as if Angela had just turned him over to the enemy or sold him out. She wanted to go get him so badly, to go pick up her man and make him well. If anything happened to him in the hospital, by any means, Angela felt that it would be her fault.

She didn't have to say a word after hanging up the phone. Christine looked sympathetic, although likely a little confused about exactly what had transpired. Endia, on the other hand, knew from her own experiences what the call had been about. Silent tears streamed down Endia's face as she seemed to search for something comforting to say, then opted instead for silence.

Angela didn't have much of an appetite after that call.

"I'm going to the car," she said, while standing up from the table, leaving a full plate of food in front of her.

"We'll all go," Christine said, standing as well. "We'll just get the food to go, so you won't have to be by yourself." Placing an arm around Angela's shoulder, Christine tried to draw her in.

"No . . . really . . . thank you . . . I just need to be alone for a minute," Angela said, pulling away gently. "Please?" Before they could answer, she was halfway to the door.

After climbing into the Expedition, Angela instinctively turned on the Fred Hammond gospel CD that usually brought her peace. *All things are working for me. Even things I can't see.* But this time, as she sang, the words felt hollow and meaningless to her, and instead of the usual sense of peace that came over her, Angela found herself angry.

"I can't do this! If this is my test, I don't want it! . . . Can you hear me?" she yelled.

"He just has to be ok! I don't know what I'd do without him. Please, please God, let him be ok. I'll do anything; just tell me what to do to make it right!" she prayed aloud.

Emotionally and physically exhausted, and not even caring if anyone was around, Angela lay her head on the steering wheel and cried out loud. She cried because she believed what they say about God never giving you more than you can bear, which meant that this mountain wasn't going anywhere until she learned how to climb it.

‖

"So, I just left him there. Like dropping a dog off at the vet or something. I didn't try taking him home, or researching good doctors to find the best one. I just left him at some hospital and hoped for the best." A tear that has been threatening to fall finally slips from the corner of my eye.

"Don't you think you're being a little hard on yourself Angela?" Mary asks.

My mind's eye holds an image of Marcus' face when he said he didn't want to stay at the hospital. Over and over again, I see his eyes pleading for me – the person who is supposed to love him the most – to do something. And I just left him.

"But he wanted me to help him, and I didn't."

"You really don't think so?"

I pause to think about the question, but come up empty. "Well, unless you count driving him to the mental hospital and dropping him off." I try not to sound as sarcastic as I feel, but don't succeed.

"Actually I do. I count everything you did to help him and to hold it together yourself."

I give Mary a dumbfounded look, but don't speak for several seconds.

"But, that's not *doing* anything. I should have done more to help him, to make sure he was ok."

"Well, let's think about what options you had. You could have lost it yourself, fallen completely apart, and checked in to the hospital too."

"Believe me, I thought about it."

"But you didn't. Things got hard and you dealt with them. Somehow, someway, you kept moving. And that's something to be proud of."

No matter what Mary says, it still feels wrong.

I sit there wondering what it would feel like to be stronger – to be the type of person who doesn't always care what other people think – kind of like Endia. That girl can throw on some camouflage pants and zebra print pumps, then have everyone convinced that it's the new style. Why can't I be more like that?

"I see what you're saying, but I don't feel proud, or strong. I'm the one who had to call my friends to come hold my hand, remember?"

"Do you think calling for support is a sign of weakness?" Mary asks, then looks at me pointedly. I look away, hoping she doesn't see how weak I feel. Hoping she doesn't know how much I really just want to crawl into bed and not get up.

"Angela, there comes a time in everyone's life when they've got to depend on someone else to make it through. That's ok. In fact, I think it's good because it helps us remember that there are some things we can't control. That even when we give it our best, stuff still sometimes happens."

I try to absorb the meaning behind her words, but my mind is already traveling back to the worst day of all.

12

"**G**OOD MORNING, ANGELA. HOW ARE YOU TODAY?" the counselor asked.

Angela hoped that her blank stare back was an answer. It was better than the truth. *How am I today? I'm about to lose my freakin' mind if you don't hurry up and take me to my husband, and if he's not sounding like the man I knew two days ago, you might have to check me in too. That's how I am . . . I'm about to need a room of my own.*

If she had looked like a bum on Friday when she picked up her girls, Angela wondered what in the world she looked like on Saturday as she walked into Peachtree Hospital on Visitors' Day. The bandana and flip-flops had worked so well that she decided to make them part of her permanent uniform. Since comfort was all that mattered, Angela completed the outfit with black leggings and a large green jersey that had the word "boundless" on it. The jersey, which usually served as lounging pj's, came down almost to her knees and seemed to swallow her up. But it felt comfortable and reminded her of better days. Usually when she put it on, the logo reminded her that there was no limit to what she could do. Unfortunately, today it hadn't been doing the trick. On this day, she felt fully and completely out of control.

The hospital looked different that morning. The waiting room was empty, and she realized for the first time that you couldn't get beyond the waiting area without being let in, typically by a counselor from the inside. When Angela had asked for the counselor on duty, they paged her, and Brenda Thomas came quickly to the front.

Brenda couldn't have been more than forty, but her eyes looked as if she'd done twice as many years of living. She had to be almost six feet tall, towering over Angela by at least a few inches. Slim. Largely nondescript. Polite, but not warm.

Taking a cue from the silence she received in response to her greeting, Brenda didn't chitchat any further. Instead, she escorted Angela back to the door behind which Marcus had disappeared two nights before. While Angela stood back hesitantly, Brenda rang the buzzer and the door opened in a matter of moments.

Once inside, Angela could see down one of the long corridors to a nurses' station in the middle. Before they reached the station, Angela and Brenda passed an open room to the right. Angela guessed that it must be a room for congregating because there were a number of folks sitting on the sofas and chairs, talking noisily. There was also a second common area behind the nurses' station, where an arrangement of neutral-colored couches accommodated another group of men and women who were talking quietly. She didn't see Marcus.

"Hey, thanks for coming to see me!" a woman who Angela had never seen before said loudly as Angela walked past.

"Huh? Uh, ma'am, I don't think we've met," Angela said, stopping to respond, seemingly unnoticed by Brenda. Without any reaction to Angela's words, the woman bounced off to talk to someone else.

Noticing that Angela had fallen behind, Brenda turned around to see what was taking so long. "Angela, it's probably best if you don't talk to the patients," she said briskly. Motioning with her hand, Brenda quickly directed Angela through the busy area and down a hallway to her office. Other than a few files on the desk, the office looked devoid of life. No personal photos. No plants. Nothing that might give anyone a clue as to who Brenda really was.

"Have a seat," Brenda said, motioning to one of the large chairs directly across from her desk. Angela sat down in the chair nearest the windows and tapped her foot nervously as she tried to relax.

A few moments later, a nurse escorted a smiling Marcus into the office. Angela noticed that he'd changed into the warm-ups that she had dropped off with the front receptionist the morning before. Other than the change in clothes, there was something else different, but Angela couldn't quite define it. There was something wrong with his smile. Just like in her dream, his lips curled upward, but the smile didn't reach his eyes, which looked empty and sad.

Angela felt bad that she couldn't recall if he'd ever looked sad like that in the past. Before she could examine her guilt, Marcus ran over and hugged her like an excited schoolboy. Angela held on to him as if her life depended on it, until the counselor cleared her throat loudly.

"I'm sorry to interrupt you, and I promise you'll have some time to visit after our session. We have a lot to cover, so I'd like to start as soon as you're ready."

Angela took her cue and moved to one of the chairs facing Brenda's desk. Though they sat separately, Marcus' eyes remained fixed on Angela. He seemed to be trying to reassure her that he was ok, but the more energy he sent her way, the more her stomach cramped in response. Unfortunately, not the kind of cramps she suddenly hoped for.

"Angela, I thought it would be a good idea if Marcus and I shared some of the things we've been talking about since he got here, and he's given me his consent to do so," she started, while putting on her glasses and opening a file in front of her. "I'm hoping that this will be a good first step toward confronting some of the things that have been bothering him and that probably led to his confusion."

Marcus reached over and grabbed Angela's hand, and began rubbing on it. Somehow the rubbing motion was making her feel nauseous.

"I just want him to get better . . . I know he's been really stressed with the business and all. He needs to learn how to relax. He's been running so much . . ." Angela stopped when she realized she was rambling.

"True, true." Brenda took off her glasses. "But let's take a step back a little farther. How much do you know about Marcus' childhood?"

"What do you mean? What does that have to do with anything?" Angela asked, not sure if she really wanted to know.

"Well, as I'm sure you could guess, most of the things we experience as adults have to do with patterns we learned as children. With Marcus, he learned a lot from his parents."

"But Marcus doesn't even know his dad," Angela said, trying to control the unexpected surge of protection she felt. Marcus' dad had never been there, and he had dealt with it.

"You're right. He doesn't know his dad. But I guess the more relevant question is what effect do you think that's had on him?"

Angela thought about how she'd always pegged Marcus as being so strong and well-adjusted, considering that he didn't even know his father's name. It was as if that became the motivating force for him to do better with his life and to do better by his future kids. Angela had always thought the effect had been positive.

"From what Marcus has told me, he was raised by his mother, who was just a kid herself. So like most children in that situation, Marcus felt like he had to be the man of the house, helping out with his younger brothers." Brenda paused to see if Angela was with her. "Because his mom was working a lot to keep things going, Marcus always felt like he was on his own. He never felt supported."

"Yeah, I know all of that, but I'm not sure where that gets us today," Angela said, growing impatient with the process, and even more nauseous as Marcus kept on with that irritating rubbing.

"Did Marcus tell you how traumatic it was for him when he found out that the man he thought of as his father really wasn't?"

"Yeah, of course." Angela wondered why she suddenly felt defensive, but she couldn't help it. She felt a subconscious pang of guilt as she wondered if this was somehow her fault for not realizing his childhood still haunted him.

"When he told me how he learned about his real dad, Marcus said it was hard finding out the truth, but that when he did, suddenly everything made sense," Angela said. "Why the man who he thought was his father treated him different from the other kids.

"Marcus told me that he felt deceived and hurt; he felt like he didn't belong to anyone. So he told his mom that he was going to go live with his aunt, and his mom didn't even ask him to stay.

"I always knew he had some hurt feelings . . . I mean, who wouldn't?" Angela asked. "But he and his mom mended the best they could. And he accepted her for who she is. What more could he do?" Angela finally paused for air, while realizing that she was more than mildly irritated by the questions, even though she knew her feelings were misplaced.

One of the things she loved most about Marcus was how well he'd overcome his circumstances. Like having a young mother to whom he clearly wasn't a high priority. In fact, Marcus talked about how he couldn't remember her attending even one of the memorable events in his life. He'd grown up feeling unloved and unwanted, so of course that had an effect on him. Yet, he persevered. After basically raising himself, he'd joined the military and then gone on to get two degrees. And he'd loved his mother in spite of it all. Doesn't that show how well he adjusted to it all?

"Did Marcus ever talk to you about how his mom would, um, entertain men when he was young?" Brenda broke character momentarily as a look of sympathy passed across her face before she again busied herself by purporting to read more of the file.

Angela wanted to pretend that she already knew. After all, she knew her man, right? But her blushing face had most likely given her away long before she finished considering the not-so-hidden meaning in Brenda's words.

Angela's silence must have been a response, because Brenda continued.

"Marcus said he'd sometimes hear her bring men home, and how much it bothered him." Sensing Angela's discomfort, she moved on quickly. "But the bigger issue is that his mother never got married. Not to oversimplify it, but his mother never trusted or committed to anyone, and now Marcus realizes that he has some of the same issues."

Angela sat there thinking about how long they had dated on and off before finally getting engaged, and how she fell in love with Marcus way before he seemed to really care. Angela had known from the first time she met Marcus that he could be the one, but he'd resisted getting attached. And since he was obligated to go back to the military after college, and didn't even know where he'd be stationed, he had a ready excuse for not settling down. But maybe there was more to it? Taking the huge chip off her shoulder and now really considering what the counselor was saying, it all made sense.

"It took a while, but we got past all that," Angela said. "And now he does trust . . . He does trust me, right?" Angela looked from the counselor to Marcus and back to the counselor. She hoped Marcus didn't think she would ever leave or betray him. Even if he was sick, they'd find a way to make it better.

Marcus had been sitting there silently, but Angela heard him clear his throat as if he were about to speak. She noticed that he wasn't smiling anymore, and she was suddenly scared.

"I'm going to leave the two of you alone to talk for a bit. Just go to the nurses' station and ask them to find me if you need me," Brenda said, and she then left the office.

Without any icebreaker, Marcus dived right in.

"Angie, I don't want to have a baby," he began.

"What do you mean?"

"The truth is I'm not even close to ready. That's one of the things that's been bothering me."

Angela instinctively rubbed on her stomach, as if protecting their possibly not-so-hypothetical child. She was at a total loss for words. *How can he just change his mind when he knows it might be too late?*

"It's not that I don't want us to have children eventually. It's just that the thought of being a parent – when I don't even have a clue what that's supposed to look like – scares the crap out of me. How can I be a good father when I've never even seen one?"

Angela's hurt feelings began to dissipate as she saw the fear in his eyes and realized where it came from.

"Baby, it's ok to be scared," she said. "Don't you know how scared I am too? One thing I've learned is that there's no such thing as a 'normal' family. I mean, look at me. My parents stayed together until Daddy died. We lived in a middle-class neighborhood. Nobody left. As far as I know, nobody cheated. Nobody went to jail or did anything crazy. From the time I was old enough to remember, nobody even drank. All we did was go to church every day of the week. But, in looking back, I can see that we were still dysfunctional– dysfunctionally perfect, that is. So I'm scared that I'll be the same way with my kids. That I won't let them make mistakes. That I'll force them to be as perfect as I tried to be . . . Every family has its issues."

"Yeah, but . . ."

"There are no buts, Marcus. It's ok to be scared. Don't you think I'm terrified that I won't be a good mother? I'm scared to death, but I know we'll be ok as long as we're doing it together."

"Angie, there's more . . ."

Summoning up peace from deep inside her, Angela looked Marcus squarely in the eye. What she saw scared her. Made her want to stop him from talking so they could go back to pretending that everything was perfect, the way it was yesterday.

"The reason why . . ." Marcus started to speak, but his voice broke as he struggled to hold back the tears. Before this episode, she had seen him cry only once in eleven years, and now, suddenly, it was as if he couldn't turn it off.

"The reason why I couldn't trust you is because I'm untrustworthy." Marcus exhaled slowly, then watched her closely without saying more.

A million feelings raced through Angela in a single second. Confusion, disbelief, clarity, disbelief, anger – all in a moment's time. *Untrustworthy?*

"Marcus, what exactly are you saying?" Angela asked, as she moved her hand away from his and stood up slowly.

13

ANGELA WAS CERTAIN SHE HEARD MARCUS' HEART beating loud and fast, but not loud enough to drown out the other thoughts that were flying through her mind at warp speed.

He couldn't be saying what she thought he was saying. He would never do that. Never. They had a good marriage. Not perfect, because there's no such thing, but a really good marriage.

Looking at his furrowed brow, however, Angela felt that she had to ask the question, even though she wasn't sure she wanted to know the answer.

"Are you saying that you cheated on me?" she asked in a soft and deceptively calm voice.

Marcus didn't say anything. He just sat there for what seemed a lifetime, and then finally, slowly nodded his head in an act of mute cowardice. Angela felt as if a knife was piercing through her as she closed her eyes and tried to find a way for it to all make sense. Had she understood him right? Yes. Had he understood her question? Yes, she thought so.

Untrustworthyuntrustworthyuntrustworthyuntrustworthy . . .

Untrustworthyuntrustworthyuntrustworthyuntrustworthyuntrust worthy.

It was the first time since her father's death that Angela could remember having something akin to an out-of-body experience. She could hear the man she'd loved for more than eleven years tell her that he didn't want to start a family – a detail he might have mentioned before possibly getting her pregnant – and then calmly admit to cheating on her, but she couldn't take it all in. She tried to convince herself that she'd heard wrong, or that it was a dream from which she'd awaken if she could only keep still, or better yet, that he was disillusioned. No, theirs had not been a perfect marriage, but she never thought he'd ever cheat. That was something that happened to women who didn't take care of their men, or couples with problems – but not to them. And those women always knew. Didn't they?

Angela needed answers. Maybe it wasn't as bad as it sounded, or perhaps it was all in his head. So she decided to ask the hard questions, and allowed her lawyerly curiosity to take over. She couldn't let him off with a simple nod of the head.

"Did this happen more than once?" Angela asked in a flat, even tone, as if she was questioning whether he took out the trash.

"Yes." He finally looked at her directly. His glazed eyes were pleading for her to understand, but he knew better than to say more at that moment. Angela felt as if someone had dealt a blow to her midsection, and she almost doubled over in pain. But she couldn't stop there. She had to know it all.

"What I meant to ask is whether you were with more than one woman, not whether there was more than one time."

After what felt like a long pause, he gave a slight, almost imperceptible nod of his head. When she kept eyeing him, Marcus opened his mouth meekly and said, "yes" in a low tone. A single tear slid down his face as he looked at Angela, still pleading. "I really don't know why I did it. I'm so sorry. I'm really sorry, Angie."

Anger battled self-pity, which battled disgust, and finally hurt as she watched her manly man melt before her eyes. Part of her felt good that he was suffering. If this was true, he deserved to suffer, didn't he?

"Last year I met this woman at a conference. Her name was Kara . . . And then there was another woman that I met at work named Danise, but that didn't last long. We only saw each other a few times . . ."

Two women in the last year alone? Were there more? Was this for real? Did she even want to know?

As much as she wanted to punish him, Angela realized that she was the only one being punished by Marcus' confessions, while he was likely feeling better at unloading his guilt. She was done with her interrogation, and didn't care if he didn't say another word.

Unfortunately, he wouldn't stop talking. It was as if he'd been given a truth serum, and suddenly needed to confess every dalliance in great detail. So, while she stood there in a daze, Marcus told her about several of the women he'd been with. With each new detail, Angela became sure that he was telling the truth and that her marriage had been something of a lie.

"And then there was Stephanie. We slept together a few times. But mostly we were just friends," Marcus added.

Although she had thought identities didn't matter, Angela's head snapped when he mentioned his old classmate from graduate school, Stephanie. His "girl" Stephanie, who he sometimes studied with, and who from time to time called the house to speak to him about an upcoming project or exam. The same girl who Angela had welcomed to call their home anytime, and who she had met on several occasions. It was always Stephanie and Lori and Marcus studying together, but Angela never imagined that someone who was in her face would be sleeping with her husband. Angela was so distracted by her thoughts that she almost didn't realize Marcus was continuing his confessions.

"And then there was Lori. . . We didn't exactly sleep together, but . . . you know."

What? Had she heard that right? So he cheated with both Stephanie and Lori? Weren't they friends?

Never in her wildest dreams would she have imagined that the women she'd befriended would be backstabbing. Angela realized that he was still talking and crying, but she was too busy thinking about those hookers coming into her house and pretending to be all friendly while cheating with her man.

Angela felt like one of those cartoons where there was an angel on one shoulder and a devil on the other. Her angel was reciting scriptures on faith and love and healing, while her devil told her to kick him in a way that would make him think about her every time he even thought about sex in the days and months to come.

Marcus continued with confessions of cheating, mostly with classmates from his MBA program, while Angela's mind clouded with thoughts of how they probably thought she was a fool. After all, while she was prancing around, trying to tell other folks how to get a good man, the joke was really on her.

Why didn't he just shut up? How could he sit there, detailing all the lies and cheating without even seeming to care how much he was hurting her? He just kept talking and crying. It was probably making him feel better to get it all out, but with every word Angela felt like another brick had been dropped on her chest.

Suddenly noticing that Angela had finally given in and doubled over with her head in her hands, he paused for the first time. "Angie, are you ok? I can't lose you, I can't . . . We can work this out."

"Just stop!" Angela said, in a louder tone than intended.

Her outburst appeared to have startled Marcus. He started sobbing at full throttle then, and Angela guessed she should have felt . . . something. But all she felt was numb, and as if she were suffocating. She couldn't stay there one second longer. In fact, Marcus was still talking as she moved toward the door. She needed to be outside where she could breathe.

"Angie, wait!" Marcus said, before she reached the door. Angela turned to look at him, certain that she must look at least 10 years older than when she'd entered the hospital an hour earlier. Something about Angela's body language must have made Marcus uncomfortable, because he shrank back before he began talking. She hoped he could see in her posture that only a thin thread kept her from losing it altogether.

Stepping back from her, Marcus' face suddenly contorted in fear. "You used to say if I cheated, you'd kill me."

"What?" Angela tried to make sense of what he was saying. "What are you talking about?" Of course she remembered half jokingly telling him, "If you ever cheated, I'd leave you. But if you cheated and brought any disease into my house, I'd have to kill you." Back then, they'd both laughed and promised to always be honest and faithful, and never to put each other at risk in any way. Was that what he was talking about?

Before she could figure out where he was going with this, Marcus' expression changed to one of intense fear and he began to yell, "Oh my God, I've given you AIDS! That's why you're trying to kill me! Is that it? I gave you AIDS?"

14

AIDS?

The television went back to mute, as Marcus continued to speak. He paced back and forth, his hands moving animatedly. The tree indentation on his head deepened and wrinkled, as his eyes moved between Angela and the empty spaces of the room.

Breathe in. Breathe out. Breathe in. Breathe out. The room tilted and the floor came closer. *Breathe in. Breathe out.* The floor stepped back away from her. *Breathe in. Breathe out.*

Angela focused on the lips that hadn't even paused for a commercial break. Tried to give meaning to the movements of his mouth. But she couldn't understand anything he was saying. Or maybe she didn't want to.

The man in front of her wasn't her husband. Her husband was calm and in control. He commanded attention when he entered a room, without saying a single word. He knew how to speak authoritatively without yelling, and how to win anyone over. He was the next Bill Gates.

No, this person before her – this shell of a man she thought she knew – was someone else, someone completely out of control.

AIDS? Oh my God! Breathe.

"What the hell are you talking about? AIDS? Do you have AIDS? Do you?" She finally found a voice, though she wasn't sure whose voice it was. This voice could break glass. This voice sounded as if the person speaking had already broken.

Time froze as she glared at Marcus, willing him to say, "no, I don't have AIDS. No, I don't think you're trying to kill me. No, I would never, ever cheat on you. This has all been a big joke. Or, better yet, a dream. You're going to wake up and tell me all about it. Then I'm going to hold you until you stop shaking and know that would never happen as long as we're together."

Instead, she heard him continue his rant, saying, "that's why you're trying to kill me, isn't it? That's why I'm here? Because I gave you AIDS?" Marcus resumed pacing back and forth in front of the desk, with a hand on his head. He looked as disturbed as she felt.

Was that a yes? Could she be HIV positive? What if she was pregnant? What about their baby?

"Marcus, please, please just answer me," she pled. "I promise I'm not trying to kill you, and I'm not going to hurt you, but I need to know. Are you HIV positive? . . . Please just tell me." It took everything in her being to keep her voice low and her tone nonthreatening. She just hoped that Marcus' normal intuition wasn't working, because if it was, he'd know what she was really thinking. If she found out that Marcus had given her the AIDS virus, she was certain that she would kill him in the cruelest way she could imagine. Slow. Deliberate. And without remorse.

"You're trying to kill me!"

"What? No, sweetie, no one is going to hurt you. Just help me understand. Did you have unprotected sex?"

Angela remained calm on the outside, but was contemplating what she would do if he said yes. Stab him in the eye with a pen from Brenda's desk? Run him over with the car? What could she possibly do to return the damage he may have caused?

"Of course not," he said. "I always used condoms. What am I, stupid?"

Angela exhaled a little bit of the breath she'd been holding, but quickly drew it back in when she realized that his words may not be true. How did she know for sure? Is it possible that she could be HIV positive even though she was married and faithful? That someone she loved and trusted could have killed her for some meaningless sex?

"I want to go home now," he continued, becoming agitated again. "I know what you're doing, and it's not going to work. I want to go home, and they can't keep me here."

"Marcus, what are you saying? You're not making any sense." Angela paused as she realized that he had been less rational during this visit than when she checked him in. Something didn't add up. It was like someone pulled the string from a hem and he just completely unraveled. Just like when he came to her building, but worse. "Wait a minute . . . Why are you talking like this? Marcus, have you been taking the medicine they gave you?"

"Of course not," Marcus said in a self-satisfied manner. "Do you think it's going to be that easy to do me in? I just pretended to take it . . . I'm not taking any medicine, and I'm going to find the doctor to figure out when I can go home."

As if on perfect cue, Brenda came back into the room before Angela could respond. Angela couldn't tell if she'd been listening in or been summoned because of the noise. She just hoped that after seeing Marcus' erratic state, Brenda would make sure that he got help.

Before Angela could say a word, Marcus turned to Brenda and spoke. "Brenda, hey, perfect timing," he said calmly and without any hint of emotion. "We were just wrapping up."

If Angela hadn't seen it with her own eyes, she wouldn't have believed it. Gone were the lines of animosity, fear, and rage that had taken hold of his face. Gone was the raised voice, and in its place was a man fully in control of his faculties.

Or, at least, a man who was really good at faking it.

"I think it's been really helpful talking to you," he started, with just the right amount of sincerity. "But I have to ask, what's the next step? I feel like I need to be at home with my wife."

Home? With her?

"Well, typically we want to meet with you several times to ensure —"

"I need to go," Angela said, interrupting her. When she saw the look of surprise on Brenda's face, she added, "I just . . . I just can't be here right now."

Before Marcus or Brenda could say anything, Angela grabbed her bag from the floor and was out the door. She didn't stop running until she reached the first locked entrance, which someone miraculously unlocked for her to exit. When she reached the second locked door, thankfully someone was waiting to let her out. Angela didn't stop running until she made it to her truck, parked in the rear of the parking lot. Once in, she found herself in familiar territory, head pressed against the steering wheel, praying a prayer that didn't have words. They say God understands all things, and she hoped it was true as her moans told him her story.

Angela prayed during the entire forty-five-minute drive back to the sanctuary of her home, and back to her girls. "Just let me get home . . . Please, just let me make it home," she murmured out loud. The drive seemed to take hours, but Angela would not let herself cry or even begin to process anything that had happened. She knew that once it was all acknowledged, she might not have the strength to get back up.

When she opened the door to her place, Endia and Christine were sitting on the couch in the front room, watching television. Angela stepped over the threshold, and opened her mouth to speak to them. But before any words could escape, her legs buckled under her. At the same time, Angela heard this horrible howling noise, which she later realized was coming directly from her.

15

UST MOMENTS AFTER ANGELA HIT THE ENTRANCEWAY'S hardwood floor, Christine was there holding her and rubbing her back in nice, round circles. Christine kept saying, "It's going to be ok," and Angela tried her best to believe it. She felt other arms around her and, without opening her eyes, could tell that Endia was at her side too.

Angela wasn't sure how long they all stayed in that weird threesome hug on the floor. Only that after a while she ran out of tears, and miraculously, God had given her more air to breathe. As her breathing gradually became more even, she felt herself coming back to the present.

When she regained the ability to speak, Angela started from the beginning. "Marcus told me . . ." she paused to figure out how in the world to say it. Saying it would make it real.

"He told me some things . . ."

Angela paused to try to gather her words.

"Marcus said the reason he couldn't trust me . . . is because . . . he's 'untrustworthy.'"

"Untrustworthy?" Christine asked innocently. "Well, what does that mean? What did he lie about?" Christine babbled on with different thoughts as Endia sat in silence.

"Are you saying what I think you're saying?" Endia asked softly.

Angela nodded, then filled them in on what had happened at the hospital. Her friends sat with looks of disbelief as she told them about the infidelity, but intentionally left out the part about AIDS and about the potential pregnancy. She wasn't ready to deal with either of those issues, and instead prayed that she wouldn't have to do so. Maybe he really did use condoms and maybe her period was just late because of stress. That was her prayer.

"I don't know what to say," Christine said, as Endia kept her silence. "This is unreal."

"I know."

Christine reached over and grabbed one hand, and Endia gently squeezed the other, which she'd been holding since Angela landed on the floor.

"I know we can't make it better," Endia said softly. "But no matter what, Angie, we're here for you."

"Yeah, girl . . . Plus, Marcus hadn't taken the medicine, so you can't believe everything he said . . ." Christine began, with her typical optimism. "And you know that God always works things out. If this had happened even a month ago when you weren't working, Marcus wouldn't have insurance . . . And think about how you could never find the right time to get pregnant. You didn't know that God was working it out for your own good then, did you? But at least you don't have kids to worry about. You're going to be ok, and so will Marcus."

Angela glanced carefully at her friends, hoping that she'd been successful in hiding her thoughts, while fearing that Endia had picked up on what she had yet to share with them. Angela had never been able to hide anything from her friend for long. It was like Endia was the one person who could see right through her.

Just as she was doing then – looking clear to her soul. She was looking at Angela in a way that most folks don't take the time to do. She was seeing her, and Angela felt exposed. Her eyes started to water again. She didn't even wait for Endia to ask the question. Just blurted it out.

"My period is late."

"Wha . . . ?" Christine gasped, while Endia closed her eyes as if her worst fears were confirmed. When she opened them, her eyes were wide and glossy. Angela took note of Endia's momentary indecision as her friend decided against asking questions. Instead she grabbed Angela and embraced her warmly.

"Babygirl, it'll be ok. No matter what happens, we're here for you." Endia rubbed Angela's back soothingly. It reminded Angela of being a child in her mother's arms.

"Have you taken a pregnancy test?" Christine asked gently.

"No, I just couldn't deal with that right now. If I am pregnant . . . And now Marcus is saying that he's not even ready for a baby. . ." She paused to let the tears fall freely. "I'm just not ready. Besides, my period will start. I'm just going to give it a couple more days."

Christine started to say something, but Endia shook her head discreetly, as if to say "let her be."

"The real problem is I just don't know what to do," Angela said. "Here's a man who cheated on me, and who has had some sort of breakdown, but yet I still don't know if I want to leave him . . . .

"I always thought it was simple," she added, pinching her lips together in the way she often did while lost in thought. "A man cheats on you, or hits you, and you pack your bags and go. Period. You'd have to be crazy to stay, right? And yet, here I am, wondering if I should go . . ."

Endia let out a deep sigh, then gave Angela a reassuring smile before responding. "Angie, this is your marriage and your husband. I can't sit here and even front like I know what it's like to be in your place . . . All I know is that you can't make big decisions overnight. You just need to take one day at a time, and figure out what's best for you in that moment. It shouldn't matter what anyone else thinks, but know that we're your girls and we'll support you in whatever you decide."

"I honestly don't know what I'm going to do."

"Well, if you decide to stay here and see if you can work it out, and help Marcus get back on his feet, you know we're with you, girl," Christine said.

"Or if you decide you want to take his behind out while he's sleeping, bury him in the backyard, and keep stepping like you don't know what happened, we'll take it to the grave. Ride-or-die, right?" Endia added, somewhat jokingly.

Angela smiled weakly and sighed, then closed her eyes to collect herself.

"But he's going to be ok, right?" Angela asked no one in particular. Christine and Endia glanced at each other, and Endia paused, apparently deciding to think before saying anything. Filling the gap, Angela added: "No matter what happens with our marriage, he's . . . well, he's my best friend. So I need to know that he's going to get through this."

"Angie, I'm sure they'll help Marcus get better . . . But you need to realize that most people aren't really the same after something like this. Any sort of a breakdown takes work to recover from. It's not going to be easy, and he's not just going to be ok overnight. For now, just try to be positive and wait to see what the doctors say."

Without any more words, the three of them resumed their spontaneous hug position there on the wooden floor. They stayed that way until Angela ran out of tears again, which was a very long time.

16

"THAT WAS ONE OF THE WORST DAYS OF MY LIFE," I say to Mary. "I just felt so alone and scared."

"Of course you were scared. Anyone would have been frightened in that situation. . . . Why don't you tell me what you felt *most* afraid of?"

I close my eyes and remember the overwhelming feeling that my life was over. The fear that nothing would ever be the same.

"I don't know. Maybe everything," I finally say, shrugging my shoulders as if to push off the weight of it all. "Sometimes I was scared of getting a divorce, and being forced to learn how to live without him. Sometimes I was scared of staying with him. I kept thinking that even if he got through it okay, how did I know that he wouldn't lie again?"

Mary doesn't say a word, but her eyes confirm that my fears are valid.

"What else?"

I close my eyes, not wanting to admit the worst of it, but knowing I have to be honest with Mary and even more, with myself.

"It's going to sound shallow, but I was also afraid of what people would think if they heard Marcus went to a mental hospital. I was afraid our friends might never look at us the same way again – that they'd treat us different because . . . that's what people do."

Mary leans in closer and looks me directly in the eye, then asks, "Is it fair to say you were afraid they would find out you weren't the perfect couple?"

"No," I say, leaning away from her. "Of course not."

"I'm just asking because that's the way you described Marcus earlier. You said you met the *perfect* man."

I smile a little, as I remember saying those exact words, and even more, feeling that way. "Maybe because part of me thought he was. Not perfect, but about as close as you can get."

"Why?"

"Why? Because I was only 18 when we met. It was my first time living away from home, and I met the most incredible guy. He was five years older; he had traveled the world; he was super smart and sexy; and he could have had any girl on campus. But he chose me."

I smile as my mind recalls the image of the first time we kissed. How my heart felt like it might beat out of my chest.

"What's so surprising about that? You're obviously pretty smart to have been a sophomore at 18, and to have gone on to law school. Now you're working at a prestigious law firm. And from looking at you, I would think you could have had any guy on campus. Am I wrong?"

I blush and roll my eyes.

"Well, am I?"

"I don't even know how to answer that. . . . I just felt like I got *the* guy."

Mary continues to peer at me intensely, but I don't look away. I must finally wear her down because she makes a note, then changes her angle.

"Angela, was Marcus' hospitalization the first time you realized there were issues?"

My turn to look away. I glance around the office searching for something to distract me, but there's nowhere to hide. I'd never known Marcus was experiencing emotional issues, but there had been signs that something was wrong. I just didn't see it.

"Angela, did you hear – "

"No." My voice is only slightly above a whisper because it's the first time I've admitted it, even to myself.

"So you knew there were issues before. Will you tell me about it?"

I nod, but take a moment to gather my thoughts. See images of me sitting in a New Orleans hotel room crying, wondering what I did wrong.

"One day about a year ago, out of the blue, Marcus told me he didn't know if we were going to make it."

"Just like that?"

"Just like that. No warning. No intro. Just like it was casual conversation. I thought we were happy, and then – I was totally caught off guard."

"Wow," Mary says, "That had to have been hard."

I nod in response. Hard doesn't even begin to describe the feeling I had when Marcus made his grand announcement midway through our vacation. One minute we were laughing and the next minute he didn't think we would make it. It was all so bizarre and sudden.

"So, I won't ask how it made you feel," Mary says, with a slow smile. "Instead, I want to know what you did about your feelings. How did you process it all?"

"What do you mean?"

"Did you cry? Scream? Throw him out of the house?"

"Cry? Yes. But, scream or throw him out? Of course not."
"Did you talk to your family and friends to try to ask for advice? Or prayers?"

"No."

"Why not?" Mary tilts her head to the side and peers at me with her eyebrows raised.

"Mostly because I didn't want anyone to know. We went to counseling and we fixed it."

Mary pauses as I stop to remember how hard it was going through that alone. The nights I'd cried wondering how I could make my marriage work.

"So, did anyone else find out after you 'fixed it'?" Mary asks.

Though I know Mary doesn't mean to be unkind, I wince slightly at the question. I had only put a bandaid on the situation, then convinced myself that I'd made things ok again. It was a sign of what was going on with him emotionally, and until now, I never had a clue.

"No one found out then. . . but eventually, everyone knew."

"And how did that make you feel?"

"How did I feel? Embarrassed. Vulnerable. And –"

"And, what Angela?"

"And, less than perfect."

17

"MRS. BENNETT PLEASE?"

"This is Angela Bennett."

"Mrs. Bennett. . .er. . . Angela, this is Dr. Alexander from Charter Hospital. I got a message from you?"

More like four messages, Angela thought, but decided not to correct him. Instead she tried to focus on how to delicately frame her question. *"Is my husband really crazy, or just a little bit off?"* Maybe that was too direct. How about, *"Can you fix him, or not?"* Hmm, that still needed work.

"Doctor Alexander, my husband has been there for 4 days, and they haven't told me much of anything. I understand you're the doctor treating him, so I was hoping to get some information."

"Oh, ok, well . . ." the doctor's voice trailed off as if he was either reviewing the file or perhaps he was eating his lunch, judging by the soft smacking she heard. She imagined him leisurely flipping through the file while munching on a sandwich, as if he wasn't dealing with something serious. She wanted to scream already at his relaxed attitude.

"Oh yeah, here we go. . . . Hmmm . . . "

Angela imagined going through the phone to choke him if he didn't answer in the next 30 seconds.

"Well, let's see — although your husband has exhibited some highs and lows, I'm not ready to diagnose him as bi-polar. It's more likely that he's been extremely depressed for some time.

Depression over a long period of time, if untreated, in some rare circumstances can actually trigger a psychotic episode."

"You're saying that depression can cause paranoia and the type of thinking he had?"

"In some cases, yes."

"Doctor Alexander, I heard what you said, but I have no idea what that means. Is my husband going to get better? Will he have to keep taking medicine? I keep going over everything in my mind, and I just don't understand what happened. One day he was fine, and the next day he thinks I'm trying to kill him."

"I understand your frustration, but these things are sometimes difficult to pinpoint. I think it's best that we remain optimistic," he said.

"Ok, but what does that mean?"

"It means that the prognosis is good. I have no reason not to expect a full recovery."

"Really?" Angela began to breathe more regularly.

"We'll give him an anti-depressant and an anti-psychotic drug for six months, along with out-patient counseling sessions to deal with the underlying causes of his depression. Hopefully, he'll learn to monitor his stress so he won't relapse, and hopefully there won't be a need for more medicine . . . At this point, let's just take it day by day and hope for the best."

"So after six months, he'll be done with the medication and therapy?"

"That's what I expect. . . . . Yes."

Angela had been practicing law long enough to read through B.S. and get straight to the point, but this time she was too tired to plow through all the maybe's and probably's and hopefully's. Instead, she latched on to the little smidgen of hope that the doctor gave her, and tucked away her fears with all the other thoughts she was avoiding. Like what to tell her job when the generic "family emergency" line grew old and what to tell

Marcus' business associates as they continued to call. And, way back in the corner, under all the other crap and whatnots was the overriding question of whether she could forgive Marcus for what he'd done – especially if she was pregnant with their child.

Every time she tried to think about the infidelity, Angela was reminded of his other issues and found herself unable to fully process her anger. She'd always thought cheating was grounds for divorce, with no exceptions, but suddenly she found herself hesitant. Could she leave the man she'd vowed before God to love forever? And, better yet, did she even want to?

"So, he can really be ok again?" Though she tried to sound strong, the crack in her voice betrayed her.

"I have no reason not to expect a full recovery."

Angela exhaled again.

"When you pick him up this afternoon, they'll give you a schedule of the out patient sessions and he'll have a list of his meds."

"Pick him up? Today? What are you talking about?"

"Oh, I thought you knew. Well, Marcus is no longer a threat to himself or anyone else, and he wants to come home, so today it is. I thought you knew."

"How would I know? I've been calling the hospital every day for information and they won't tell me anything! And now you tell me that you're letting him go?"

"Our policy is to hold patients who are a threat to themselves or others, or who sign themselves in, for 72 hours."

"But Dr. Alexander, he's not ready. Just two days ago, he thought I was trying to kill him! He's been better since he got on the meds, but that's only been a couple of days!"

"I'm sorry Angela, but legally we can't hold someone without their consent if they're not a danger to anyone. Surely you understand the legal issues. If he wants to go home, there's nothing else we can do."

The despair in Angela's heart was so deep that she didn't know what else to ask. "So what now?"

The silence that came in response to her question told Angela everything she needed to know.

Endia and Christine prayed with Angela after she got off the phone and again when she dropped them off at the airport. Angela kept that prayer going as Brenda brought Marcus into the visitor's room. She already had her speech planned to convince Marcus to stay in the hospital a few more days. It was only Monday; he clearly needed more time to deal with everything. How could she bring a man home who just recently thought she was trying to kill him? Plus, even if he was better emotionally, Angela still wasn't sure what she wanted to do about their relationship. She needed more time.

As Marcus came through the door, Angela saw a smile start in his eyes when he saw her. He came to her slowly – somewhat cautiously, but all the while his eyes told her that he'd missed her. His eyes looked like the man she'd married.

Though she was still angry and hurt, her relief outweighed every other emotion. She didn't reach out to him, but she also didn't try to step away before he pulled her close. He hugged her as if she was fragile cargo, lingering to inhale her scent and to rub the nape of her neck. Angela enjoyed a moment of closeness before coming to her senses. She pulled away, noting that it wasn't as hard as she expected to let go. Maybe next time would be even easier.

Angela opened her mouth to tell him all the reasons he needed to stay in the hospital longer, but before she could begin, he put his finger to her lips to gently silence her.

"Angela, before you say anything, I just want you to know how sorry I am," Marcus said, staring through her eyes and into her soul. "What I did was wrong; but what was even worse was the way that I told you. I don't want to hide anything from you anymore. I don't want to try to do it all on my own. I don't care if it takes me the rest of my life – I want to make all of this up to you."

"Marc–"

"Angie, please, let me finish," he started again. "I know you don't have any reason to trust me now. I know that. But I love you more than anything, and I'm prepared to do the work. Whatever it takes to get myself together and to get us back together. That's why I asked the doctor to let me go home. I feel as if every day I stay here gets us farther from each other. I can't even focus on getting my head together while I'm thinking about you – wondering if you're at home packing. I want to come home and work on us."

Angela tried not to let the words sink in. After all, this was a man who had lied to her for years. Why should this time be any different? Why should she trust him now, when he'd given her no indication that he was trustworthy?

"Also, although I don't think there was any risk since I was always safe, I got an HIV test and it was negative. I'm sorry I put you through that and that I talked to you that way."

Although she knew that didn't completely eliminate the risk, Angela thanked God for the good news. Maybe, just maybe there was hope after all, but only if he stayed and got the help he obviously needed.

"Marcus, I want you to stay here and focus on getting you well. Don't worry about us right now. Can you do that? I promise I won't make any decisions about us until you're out of here. Ok?"

"No," he said, grabbing Angela's hands. "I need to be with you. I need to be at home. I know at home I can do better than in some strange place with all sorts of crazy folks. I feel like I'm going to crack for real if I stay here one more day."

"But Marcus, they can help you here. I just want you to stay until you're really ok."

Marcus reached out and caressed her cheek softly, staring deep into her eyes. "Just give me a chance to make things right."

"But Marc –"

"Please . . . please, Angie, take me home."

PART II

"Picking up the Pieces"

18

'M STANDING BY THE WINDOW IN MARY'S OFFICE pretending there's something interesting outside because I can't stand the look of pity in her eyes. Compassion I can handle, but pity is a different thing altogether. I don't want or need it.

My eyes search for something – anything – to take me away from this moment. The cars passing on the street. The fallen leaves. Finally, the cracked sidewalk.

For whatever reason, the sidewalk reminds me of my childhood and the house I grew up in. I called it cozy, although it was way smaller than my current home and housed three times as many people. But, if nothing else, there was always an abundance of love.

I miss the feeling of being loved, protected, and safe.

"What are you thinking about?" Mary finally asks.

"Just random thoughts," I say, unable to articulate my feelings. During the pregnant pause that follows, I hear Mary scribbling on her notepad. Before she can speak, I anticipate her next question.

"When Marcus begged me to take him home, he sounded so much like the old Marcus that I thought – I hoped – he was ok. And I decided I couldn't just leave him there.

"All this time, I thought I was doing the selfless thing. I thought I was taking care of him. But, looking back now,

I'm not so sure. Maybe I was really looking out for myself because I couldn't handle the thought of being without him."

I turn around to face Mary, expecting to see the disgust I feel mirrored in her eyes. Instead, all I see is understanding. Mary is silent for a few moments, before finally saying the words I didn't know I needed to hear.

"At that moment, you made the decision that was best for you and Marcus," she says evenly. "No one is judging you for that, and no one can tell you what you should have done. You made the best decision for you and that's all that matters."

I try to let Mary's words sink in; try to allow their meaning to erode away the self judgment I've been carrying around for months, but for some reason I can't.

"What do people think of a woman who stays with a cheating husband?" I ask. I almost choke over the word "cheating," but manage to get it out without breaking down.

"Aw, there it is again - what people think," Mary says, then pauses dramatically. "What I want to know is who are these people that we're so concerned about?"

The corners of my lips turn up slightly as I imagine these nameless, faceless blobs throwing stones at me. Then, I think of the friends who love me, and remember how they have always supported me unconditionally. Finally, I shrug my shoulders, unable to explain how they have tortured me in my mind.

"Are these people in any way affected by the decisions you make?"

"No," I say.

"Then excuse my language, but why the hell do we care what they think?"

There it is. A full smile. Why do I care so much?

"Angela, my number one concern is you. Not what some people may or may not think. Not what some people may or may not want. But you. What you want and think. And what makes you happy.

"Do you know what that is?"

What makes me happy? I ask myself, as my smile quickly fades into the worry lines that have become the norm. The question is foreign. It has been a long time since I thought about what I want. I don't even know where to begin.

Looking at the angels on Mary's table, the answer finally comes to me. The strange naysayers in my mind won't like my answer, but I can only express what I have always known, before and now.

"It's always been Marcus that makes me happy," I say.

Mary gets a look I can't decipher. I'm not sure if she's thinking it's a weak response – joining in with the faceless blobs in my head – or if she understands.

I tune out the voices that tell me my answer is wrong, thinking instead of how good it felt when Marcus came home. How, despite everything that had happened, I still wanted and needed him. How I felt, even at our worst, that we could heal anything, including the broken pieces in him and in our marriage.

19

MARCUS GENTLY ROLLED ANGELA OVER TOWARDS him so they were facing each other in bed. Slowly and softly he kissed the tears on each of her cheeks, as if the magic of his touch could wipe away the need for crying. Then he brushed her face with the back of his hand as he looked into her eyes and simply said, "Baby . . . I am so sorry."

Tears streamed down his face and mixed with Angela's as they lay there for several minutes in silence. Just being in that moment. Together.

I'm sorry . . . . No way those words could erase all of the damage he'd done. No way they could make up for the hurt and fear Angela had felt those past few days while he was in the hospital, or restore confidence that they would be ok. That would take a miracle.

But then again, Angela had already witnessed one. Seeing her husband – looking deep into his eyes and knowing that at that very moment he was there with her. In that moment, he was at peace and whole. Not arrogant like the old model, more fragile and vulnerable. But it was her man.

It was her man who had spent the drive from the hospital talking to Angela about his thoughts and fears, many of which she'd never heard before. After they got home, Angela then listened in surprise as Marcus called his mom to tell her about the hospitalization and to share some of the things about his childhood that he'd started processing in therapy. Though it didn't sound like his mom accepted any of the responsibility for how he felt, Angela admired the fact that Marcus had talked openly and honestly, and appreciated that his mom at least pretended to listen. It was a huge step for him, and hopefully would go a long way towards his healing.

No, the man who lay before her was not the same one she married, but just maybe he had the makings to become a better one.

"When I dropped you off at the hospital, I thought —" Angela paused to collect herself, "I thought you'd never be ok again. And now, I don't know what to feel. On one hand, I'm so relieved to have you here. But I'm also really confused . . . It just hurts so much." The last words trailed off as her tears increased.

"I know, baby. You have every right to hate me. But, I'm here, and I'm fighting for us. Just please, please give me another chance to make everything right."

Angela's heart rate increased, as he hesitantly moved in towards her. It reminded her of a decade before when he'd kissed her for the very first time, on the steps in front of her college dorm. His kiss had felt familiar, as if they'd done this a hundred times before and might do it a thousand times more.

In this moment, staring into the eyes of a man she had loved forever and a day, Angela wanted nothing more than to feel his lips again and to remember what it was like to come together as one. When she didn't pull away, Marcus kissed her softly, then with a sense of urgency, as if she were his last lifeline. Little by little, her body relaxed into his embrace. With each kiss, she felt some of the tension of the prior few days subside. This was her husband, the man she'd planned to grow old with. Possibly the father of her baby.

Angela told herself that she would heal Marcus and their marriage with her love. With each touch, she imagined her energy seeping into him and reshaping all that had been broken. She saw her love filling the empty spaces, and mending him in a way that only a wife can.

And all the while, as she was healing him, Angela imagined that he was doing the same for her in return.

Four hours later, Angela opened her eyes in full, finally giving up any pretense of sleep. She glanced at the clock on the night-stand and saw that it was not even 3 a.m. Slowly and carefully, Angela unwrapped her leg and arm from Marcus' body and moved her head from the nook of his neck. She then peeled back the comforter and eased quietly out of bed. Angela didn't dare look back until she'd reached the doorway, and only a brief glance then to make sure Marcus was still sleeping. Relieved that he was, she pulled the door closed and walked quickly down the hallway to the guest room.

As she lay on top of the comforter on the guest room bed, hugging a pillow tightly, Angela tried to make sense of what had happened. Had she really picked up Marcus from the hospital, come home and made love to him as if nothing had happened? Part of her was disgusted that she gave in so easily, while the other part was just relieved to have a moment she'd feared was gone forever.

He had sounded so sincere in his repeat apologies for the infidelity, and he had taken a really big step by calling his mom to have an earnest conversation about ways in which she had hurt him. But, was it really enough? Was there any way to erase the hurt he'd caused and to repair their marriage?

Plus, what if Angela was pregnant? What if they weren't in the clear for HIV?

What if life was never the same?

20

FOR THE NEXT FEW DAYS, ANGELA TRIED NOT TO think. Instead, she kept her mind focused on the essentials. Watching Marcus take his medicine each morning, dropping him off at out-patient therapy, going to the office where she pretended to work for a half day, picking Marcus up from therapy, cooking food that neither of them ate, pretending to do the work she didn't get to finish at the office, then climbing onto her side of the bed – with as much space between them as possible. After the day was done, she would fall into a restless sleep, then wake up to do it all over again.

This morning had been no different, but for some reason, as Angela sat in her office behind closed doors, she couldn't turn off her thoughts. The legal brief she was supposed to be editing sat open to the same page she'd stopped on the prior afternoon and somehow the silence sounded too loud.

It was only 8:35 a.m., and was an hour earlier in Chicago, but Angela picked up the phone in her office anyway. She drummed her fingers on the desk impatiently, as she waited for Endia to answer.

"Hey," Endia said, sounding groggy when she finally answered. "You ok?"

"Hey girl," she said, hoping Endia wouldn't notice the subtle dodge of her question.

"What's going on? How are you?"

"I'm just taking it one moment at a time like you told me to. . . . But, it's hard. Feels like I'm just going through the motions."

The line was silent for a moment, as Angela hoped her friend could read in all the things she didn't have the strength to say.

"When do you guys start marriage counseling?"

"Soon. I've got to get us an appointment."

"Well, don't put it off too long," Endia said. "And, what about the test? Have you taken it yet?"

The Test. Endia was referring to the pregnancy test that she'd bought before she left. Angela kept saying she would take it, but somehow the simple act of peeing on a stick seemed like too much.

"I'm not going to take it," Angela finally said.

"What?"

"Calm down. I don't mean I'm not going to take a test at all. I just decided that I'd rather go to a clinic. I'm going to try to go this afternoon before I pick up Marcus. A test at the clinic will be more accurate. Plus, I don't know what I'll do if – you know."

Endia gasped. "Are you saying –"

"All I'm saying is that I need to consider all my options, Endi."

"But –"

"Options, Endi. That doesn't mean I've made any decision. Options."

Angela heard Endia's thoughts in the silence that followed. She knew her friend, and understood without her saying it that she'd be against terminating the pregnancy. She would say that they didn't know the purpose of this child, and she'd also explain how little doctors know about the genetic disposition for mental illness. But, when it was all said and done, she'd support Angela in whatever decision she made, because that's what sister-friends do.

"I'll talk to you later, girl," Angela said, before Endia launched into any rebuttal.

"You promise to call me before you decide anything?"

"Yes, ma'am."

"Ok. Love you"

"Love you too."

As Angela quickly hung up the phone, she felt her heart rate quicken. It was too early for most folks to panic, but for a woman whose period came like clockwork every 27th day, even a few days late was nothing to joke about.

Angela tried not to be nervous, but her shaking hands betrayed her true feelings, as she typed in credentials to unlock her computer. *She couldn't have a baby now, could she?* Not with everything going on.

God, I want a baby more than anything, but I want to be able to shower him or her with love, and bring them into a house of love. Please, God, don't let me be pregnant now.

Please, please, please don't let me be pregnant now.

Looking around the waiting room at the clinic flooded Angela with a lot of unpleasant memories. More than a decade before, she'd sat in a similar office, with the same thoughts. When they'd finished sucking the life out of her, with what she'd envisioned to be a huge vacuum cleaner, she'd prayed for forgiveness and sworn never to find herself in that predicament again. She'd been a seventeen year-old child, who never imagined that a condom could break the first time she had sex. Angela had blamed youth and inexperience, and told herself that abortion was the only choice because she was too young to have a baby.

Maybe none of her excuses were valid, but at the time, it had felt like her only choice. Back then she'd promised God never again would she so carelessly throw away a miracle. And, yet, here she was again, wondering if she might go back on her word. Wondering if God would forgive her again.

"Angela?" the practitioner said, motioning for her to come back to an exam room. Taking a deep breath, she picked up her belongings and walked into the room.

While undressing for her exam, Angela found herself marveling at how quickly things change. Just a few weeks before, she and Marcus had a nice romantic dinner. According to Marcus, Angela had "put her foot in" the t-bone steak she'd broiled, complemented with loaded baked potatoes and a fresh spinach salad. They'd eaten dinner to their favorite jazz cd, Hypnotic, by a local artist named J-Fly, while drinking way too many glasses of red wine and talking about everything and nothing. They'd even joked about how far they'd come since the year before when they'd gone to marriage counseling, and Angela didn't have a clue that anything was wrong.

"Do you remember this song?" Marcus had said, as he stopped the jazz and put in an old cd. "Show Me" blared through their home entertainment system, and Angela had begun to smile and reminisce. It was the very first song they'd danced to a decade before at a going away party for one of her friends. Her friend had suggested that they dance, and one dance led to a night full of getting to know each other. The first time he held her in his arms, Angela knew she wanted more.

Remembering their early dates, Angela had walked over to Marcus in their living room, and kissed him. As one kiss led to more, she felt in her heart that their love was making the baby they'd always dreamed of.

How could something so right a few weeks before, suddenly feel so wrong?

It felt like hours, but was probably no more than thirty minutes before the doctor gave me the results.

"Your pregnancy test was negative," she said, smiling widely. "You are definitely not pregnant."

"But . . . I'm never late . . . ." Angela paused to gather herself as tears unexpectedly began to fall down her cheeks.

"I'm sorry, Mrs. Bennett, I thought this was the news you hoped for," she said, obviously puzzled. "But you're still young. You can always try again. . . . Just make sure you follow-up with your regular doctor if your cycle doesn't resume soon. Many times when this happens it's just caused by stress, and things go back to normal in no time."

Angela nodded quickly, embarrassed at the unexpected surge of emotions. She didn't know what was going on with her. This was what she'd wanted. Right?

As she gathered her belongings and walked quickly out of the office, Angela tried to figure out why she felt so down, then it hit her squarely between the eyes as she spotted a young couple walking through the lobby.

The man had his arm casually draped around the woman's shoulders as they waited on the elevator. Then, as Angela observed from afar, she saw the woman give her man "The Look." It was a look that made Angela's heart warm and made her sad at the same time. It was like the elevator scene in Jerry Maguire when the hearing impaired man signed "you complete me" to the woman, and you knew it was a perfect picture of love. Angela remembered when she and Marcus spoke that language, and she feared they'd lost it forever.

Angela had thought she was deathly afraid of being pregnant, but now she realized that not being pregnant was just as frightening. There was nothing to keep her in the marriage.

And, worse, there was no evidence left of the love they once shared.

21

URING THE DRIVE HOME THAT AFTERNOON, Marcus kept trying to get Angela to talk, but she said little beyond polite responses. She needed time to process everything that had happened, and wasn't quite ready to tell him about her secret trip to the clinic or to explain her mixed emotions at the results.

Angela parked their car in the driveway, then walked back to get the mail as Marcus continued on into the house. She told herself that she was taking a moment to enjoy the feel of the brisk air on her cheeks, but the truth was that she didn't want to go in.

When she could delay no longer, Angela slowly opened the door to their house, took off her jacket, and began sorting through the mail. It was mostly junk and bills, plus a plain white envelope addressed to Marcus. She dropped the pile of mail onto the table and started towards the bedroom. Then, for no reason she could ever explain, Angela went back to the table and picked up the letter with Marcus' name on it. She fingered the edges of the envelope, then decided to open it.

Dear Marcus, I was really upset to get your voice message, Angela read, then dropped the letter onto the table, unable to move – unable to read it or process the words.

Seconds passed without her moving; without her so much as taking a breath. She told herself that it was going to be ok and picked up the letter from where she'd dropped it on the table. She tried once again to read it, but the words seemed to run together. She didn't know if it was because of the tears that came out from where they'd been resting right beneath the surface, or a protective mechanism of her mind, but she couldn't for the life of her get past "Dear Marcus."

Angela blinked her eyes several times, then made herself try again.

> Dear Marcus,
>
> I was really upset to get your voice message, telling me that you told Angela about us and asking me not to call you again. How could you be so cold as to just dismiss me on a voice mail?

The words turned into an undecipherable blob of ink on the page as her eyes again filled with tears. Angela closed them and took a few deep breaths, then tried once more, this time reading more slowly.

> Did you even consider my feelings when you decided to tell Angela? Did you at least help her understand that 99% of the time, we really were just friends, and that near the end, something more grew? I don't want her to think that I'm the type of woman who would just jump into bed with someone else's husband. It's not like I meant to fall in love with you. I knew it was wrong, but it was just one of those things that happened. Now I find myself wondering if I ever meant anything to you at all.
>
> I tried leaving messages on your cell phone, but haven't heard back from you. And, the last time I called it seemed that the number was disconnected. Please call me. We need to talk. You owe me that much. And I still love you.
>
> Stephanie

Angela read the letter from beginning to end, then read it again just to be sure that she'd absorbed everything. When she had all but memorized it, Angela folded the letter and placed it back in the generic envelope it had come in. She wasn't even sure what had made her open it, since she normally didn't open mail addressed to Marcus. But now that she had, there was no going back.

Somewhere in the back of her mind, the infidelity hadn't been fully real before. Yes, he'd confessed; and yes, part of her had believed him. But the other part had silently hoped that just maybe it wasn't all real. Or, at least that it wasn't as bad as it seemed. But, here *she* was writing and throwing around words like "love," as if *she* had the right to use them.

Where did they go wrong? When he'd questioned whether they could make it, did that mean he had found someone else he wanted to be with? Were there other warning signs she had missed?

The thought jolted her out of paralysis. Driven by some undefined momentum, Angela practically ran to the family room and started throwing DVDs out of the entertainment center. The answer had to be there. Something she should have seen. It was all her fault. When they stood before a crowd of five hundred plus guests, encircled by nine brides-maids and groomsmen, and said 'I do," there wasn't a doubt in her mind that she'd meant forever; that she'd meant in sickness and in health, forsaking all others. But maybe he never did.

Angela found the DVD she wanted, then put it in and watched as it began to play. On the screen she saw a younger, more innocent version of herself. She had on a white, designer, form-fitted wedding gown, with gold embroidered thread that made her look almost regal. Her eyes looked pure and optimistic in a way that she wished she could believe they might appear one day again. She was preparing to walk down the aisle and she looked really, truly happy.

The next scene flipped to Marcus preparing for the ceremony.

"I'm really, really excited because today I'm finally marrying my best friend." Marcus' image, decked in a black tuxedo and bowtie, smiled at Angela from the television screen. His eyes were aglow and he looked genuinely excited.

"What do you think Angela is thinking right now?" the unseen videographer asked.

Marcus' image on the screen nearly bowled over with laughter, then said "Oh, that's easy. . . . She's probably thinking, what took you so long?"

Angela was so engrossed in the wedding video that she didn't see Marcus come into their family room. He quietly walked over and sat beside her on the couch, then watched her as she continued to watch the television. She knew he was watching, but wouldn't look at him. She sat there, still in her black pants suit from work, while watching their wedding video as if it were the evening news.

Without breaking her stare at the screen, Angela finally spoke to him.

"I used to think that if we ever started having problems, I'd just pull out this video to remind me of how it was in the beginning. Ya know? But, now, I'm realizing the problem isn't remembering how we started." Angela paused dramatically, then continued, "It's trying to figure out where it went wrong."

She turned to look him squarely in the eye, then asked, "Can you answer that?"

Marcus seemed at a loss for words. He probably figured that no matter what he said it would just piss her off more. Seeming to opt for honesty, he finally spoke.

"I'm what went wrong," he said softly.

Angela was startled at his response. Since he'd been out of the hospital, Marcus was frequently quiet and more reserved than she'd ever seen. Instead, he seemed to often be in a world of his own, lost in thoughts that he often chose not to share. His candor now was refreshing, but not enough to thaw her in full.

Angela needed answers, but she wasn't even sure of the question.

"One of your girlfriends sent you a note," she said, her words a hint above a whisper, as she practically threw the letter at him.

"What?" His look of confusion quickly changed to shame and disbelief as he read it.

"What right does she have to write to our house Marcus? Can you tell me that?" Angela asked, her voice level escalating. "How dare *she* feel betrayed? Seriously?"

"Then she throws in that line about not being the type to cheat. What the hell does that mean? That's like – that's like me saying I'm a vegetarian, while munching on a pork chop!"

Marcus just sat there with his mouth slightly open; looking like he wanted to speak but couldn't quite figure out how to calm the situation.

"Seriously Marcus?" she asked, adding extra emphasis just to make her point.

"Well – I –" Marcus started.

"—What does *she* know about what it feels like to put all of your trust in someone? To believe that if you take care of them they won't hurt you or let you down?

"What does she know about staying with a man who ripped your heart out," she looked directly at Marcus, "so you can help him put his life back together – helping him be ok, even when it's killing you? Does she know that kind of love?" Though Angela had gone up to level ten, the last words weren't much more than a whisper.

When she finally paused to catch her breath and realized that she'd run out of words, Marcus sat in the corner looking stunned and speechless. He started to reach out for her, but then seemed to think better of it.

"I could say I'm sorry a thousand times," he started, "but I can't change what happened, Angie. I wish I could, but I can't."

Angela didn't respond. She just stood there with her eyes closed, trying not to lose it any more than she already had.

"I'm trying to make things right," he continued. "That's why I called her, to make sure she knows it's over."

"I love you more than anything," he said, then paused a second before continuing. "Please, just give me another chance. A *real* chance, not just going through the motions like you've been doing."

It was true. Monitoring her emotions over the past few days since he'd been out of the hospital had been like watching a ping-pong game. One minute she couldn't see life without him, and wanted to support his recovery. The next minute she wanted to get in the car and just drive away. Anywhere.

Marcus seemed to want to say more, but instead reached for her hand. The pause for some strange reason reminded Angela of when Marcus had gotten down on one knee in front of her family and proposed. He said it had seemed like years went by before she nodded her head to accept his proposal. Instead of mere years, this time probably felt like centuries, as she stood in their family room contemplating what to do next.

"I need some space," she blurted out, taking her hand out of his and heading down the hallway that led to the door. As an afterthought, she grabbed her purse and jacket from the couch. "I can't be around you right now."

"But Angie . . ." he said, reaching out towards her.

Angela said nothing, while moving beyond his grasp. She walked quickly out of the house, not sure where she was headed.

22

NGELA DIDN'T KNOW WHERE SHE WAS GOING, BUT instinctively sensed that she needed a real shoulder to cry on. No slight on Endia, but this time she wanted someone who had been around long enough to have seen it all. Pulling out her cell phone as she climbed into the truck, Angela quickly pressed "1" and hit "talk." Forget what the family might think. Forget the conversation she wasn't really ready to have. It was time.

"Hello?"

"Hey Mom . . ." she said, "It's me."

"Angie? . . . Hey, baby, I was just thinking about you. I'm glad to hear your voice. I tried to call you yesterday. . . . Or maybe it was the day before. . . . I don't know. I swear the older I get, the faster time goes by." Her mom chuckled softly.

"Really? I didn't get a message from you." Angela struggled to keep her tone light and carefree.

"Now you know how I hate voicemail," her mom said. "I figured I would just call you later, but somehow it slipped my mind. . . . Hey, is something going on at work? You don't sound like yourself."

"No, work is pretty normal," Angela said, struggling to keep her tone even, while wondering how in the world to broach the subject.

"Well, what's wrong?"

"Why do you think something's wrong, Mom?"

She heard her mother sigh before responding. "Angie, I know you. What is it?"

Angela cleared her throat and tried to will herself not to cry.

"Well Mom, it's Marcus. . . ." Despite Angela's best efforts, her voice began to shake.

"Angie, you're starting to scare me, so please just tell me. Whatever it is, it'll be ok."

"It's . . . well . . . Marcus. . ." *Shoot, I already said that.* "He was really . . . stressed . . . and he checked himself into a hospital for a few days."

"Oh my God, Angie! When did this happen? Is he ok now?"

Angela quickly summarized the sequence of events with minimal detail about the paranoia and without any mention of the infidelity. She wasn't sure she was ready to share everything yet.

"Why didn't you call me from the hospital?" she asked. "You know I would have come down there. Dear God, it's just like the dream —"

"Mom, I don't want to talk about that," she said, more forceful than intended.

"But Angie —"

"No, Mom, really. It's not going to help anything. You're going to tell me that God is using this as a test to make me stronger. Right? Well, what if I don't want it?"

"Angie, you don't mean that."

"Maybe I do. This isn't fair," she said, fully giving in to tears, and then decided to blurt out everything before she lost her nerve. "And, there's more. . . . He . . . While he was in the hospital, Marcus told me he cheated on me. And now he wants another chance. I'm actually sitting in the car in the driveway because I don't want to go back into the house to face him. I just don't know what to do."

"Oh baby . . . I'm so sorry . . . I'm here for you. I just wish you hadn't been going through all this by yourself." Her mother's voice cracked and made Angela wonder if she was crying too. "But, you can't just decide you don't want to grow. When I told you about that dream, it's because it felt so real. I actually heard a voice in my dream saying –"

"I know, I know Mom, *God is going to bring you to a place of brokenness*. It's been playing over and over in my head."

"That's right. But I also heard that through it, you're going to learn your true strength. And your marriage is going to be a ministry for others."

"I remember," Angela said. "But, this can't be related. How can a cheating husband be any kind of ministry?"

"Baby, I don't mean to make light of what you're going through, but you're not the first woman to get cheated on, and you won't be the last."

"I know. . . . But I just never thought it would happen to me."

"And I *hoped* it never would. . . . Angie, I'm sorry. I really am. I hate that you – and Marcus – have to go through this," she said. "But one thing you have to realize is that nothing is perfect. Not marriage, not Marcus, and not even you. Do you hear me?"

". . . I hear you."

"Anyway, I'll be praying for both of you. And you know that if you change your mind, I can come down any time."

"But, Mom, what should I do?" Even to Angela's ears her own voice sounded twenty years younger.

Angela heard her mom inhale deeply, obviously collecting her thoughts. Even though she couldn't see her, Angela could envision her mom standing in the kitchen with her lips pinched together and head shaking back and forth as she decided what, if anything, to say.

"Oh Angie, I wish I could tell you, but I can't. I can say that anyone who knows you two knows how much you love each other. I can also tell you that God's promises don't lie."

"But how do I know what's right?"

"Well, maybe you start by realizing that there's no wrong decision, as long as you're prayerful. There's no way around this. You've got to go through."

Angela pinched her lips together in resignation, then rolled her eyes at the phone as she realized that her mom's response was no surprise. "I guess I knew that, but I was still hoping."

"Just remember that as low as you feel right now, you are going to be just fine. Actually, you're going to be better than fine. Do you hear me?"

"Yes," she replied softly.

"I love you baby."

"I love you too Mom."

When she finally hung up the phone, Angela felt a little better. Something about talking to her mom had made the burden feel lighter.

Glancing out of the truck window, she was surprised to see Marcus standing on the sidewalk not far away. She rolled the window down and waited expectantly.

"Ready to talk?" he asked, with eyes that looked hopeful she would agree. "If you need some more space, that's cool. I just wanted to make sure you're alright."

"I guess I'm as ok as I'm going to be." Angela stepped out of the truck and stood directly in front of Marcus.

"Oh . . . well . . . I'm not sure what to say," he told her, "but it was killing me to just sit inside the house, wondering if and when you were coming back. Then I just happened to look out the window and see you out here."

"Marcus . . ." she began, "what you said before was right. . . . It's not healthy for us to keep going around in circles."

Marcus inhaled deeply as he waited patiently for her to continue.

"I've just been trying to figure out how to stop. So, I called my mom."

A look of shame passed across Marcus' face. "You told her everything?"

"Yep."

He bowed his head in full surrender before responding. "So, is she driving down here to kill me?" he asked, which made Angela bite her lip to keep from smiling. It was the closest he'd come to sounding like his old jovial self since the hospital. Before she knew it she was smiling in full, followed by a small giggle. Marcus cautiously smiled back at her and she felt some of the tension ease.

"Nah, not yet at least," Angela finally said. "She told me that there's no way around this, only through.

"I know if I'm staying, I have to let go of the past. I just don't know how – how do I get to the point where it doesn't hurt?"

Marcus' eyes glistened with unshed tears. He grabbed her hand and held it, looking hopeful when she didn't pull away.

"Baby, I don't have all the answers," he said, while rubbing the back of her hand. "But I promise if you try, I'll spend the rest of my life making this up to you. I will."

Though she wasn't sure how she felt about prophetic dreams and the like, Angela couldn't deny the eerie timing of everything. Plus, there was no denying how much she loved this man. She had to see this through.

"Ok," she said, her words just above a whisper and her eyes toward the ground.

Marcus must have been holding his breath, because she felt him let out a huge sigh of relief. He reached out his free hand to touch her face gingerly, then raised her chin so that he could look into her eyes.

"No more secrets. No more lies. No more of the past. Ok?"

Angela nodded her head, as she prayed that somehow her mother was right and that there was something better on the other side of through.

23

"THAT WAS A HUGE MOVE ANGELA," MARY SAYS.

"What do you mean?"

"Do you know how many people I counsel every day who keep one foot in and one foot out of the marriage for years before figuring out how to deal with infidelity?

I suck my teeth in response. If they made a card for this occasion, what would it say "Happy Forgive Your Cheating Husband Day?"

"I think you give yourself too little credit," she continues. "You see the hard decision is not whether to stay or leave. I think the hard decision is whether to *really* stay or *really* leave. That is, if you leave, to decide you're letting go in full and are open to love again. Or, if you stay, to decide that you're going to let go of the past and give your marriage everything you've got to try to make it work. In my opinion, there's no wrong decision except indecision."

I focus on Mary's words thinking of how much they sounded like my Mom's advice. But it was still hard not to beat myself up. When I was younger, I always thought that I'd leave a man who cheated on me without even a backwards glance. But, to really execute – to leave someone who you love and who you know loves you – I learned that that's harder than I could have ever imagined.

"I think anyone who tells you that they wouldn't at least consider trying to fight for their marriage is either lying to you or lying to themselves," Mary says. "Life just isn't that black and white."

I ponder that for a minute.

"But it's really hard," I finally say. "Even though I decided to stay, I never knew how hard it would be. Every time I see women now, I'm silently measuring them up. Thinking about what they have that I don't and vice versa. Trying to figure out my value as compared to theirs. I know it's wrong, but I can't seem to stop. How do I stop feeling so – insecure?"

"First, you tell yourself that in all God's earth, there is only one you, and no one else can be youer than you."

I smile because it sounds like a riddle.

"And second?"

"Second, you cut yourself some slack. It isn't easy to realize that our mates are imperfect mortals who sometimes fail. It takes time to heal from that, and there's no rushing the process."

"Ok, two good points. And third?"

"Who said there was a third?" Mary says.

Much to my surprise, I am laughing.

I am laughing.

24

S THEY SAT IN THE MARRIAGE COUNSELOR'S OFFICE a few days later, Angela was cautiously optimistic. Glancing at the degree from Harvard on the wall of his office, Angela saw that Dr. Rogers had been a psychologist for at least fifteen years. And, judging from the plush, oversized chairs and expensive décor in his office, he must be pretty good at it.

"So, how did you two end up married?" Dr. Rogers asked after they finished with introductions.

"Well, we dated on and off through college," Marcus said. "But honestly, I wasn't trying to get tied down. I'd already committed to going back to the military after school, and I didn't even know where I'd be stationed. Marriage was the last thing on my mind."

"So, what happened?"

"In our last year of school, Angie just starting doing things to show she had my back. She even threw me a birthday party. . . . Even though we didn't plan to keep seeing each other after graduation, she was always there. That's really the bottom line. For the first time in my life, I felt like someone was really there for me." Marcus smiled, but the smile wasn't wide enough to hide the pain in his eyes.

Angela didn't say anything, but thought back on the birthday party she'd thrown for Marcus shortly before they graduated.

Who would have guessed that a home-cooked lasagna and Italian cream cake would be the turning point in their relationship? It wasn't until later that Marcus admitted it was the first time anyone had ever thrown him a party, even as a kid.

"So, did you two decide to get married after graduation?"

"Not right away. But that's when I finally knew I couldn't run anymore," Marcus said, looking at Angela with a hesitant smile. "And three years later, while she was in her last year of law school, that's when we got married."

Dr. Rogers nodded at Marcus, then turned his attention to Angela.

"You've been pretty quiet, Angela. Why don't you tell me about your marriage? Before recent events, would you say that you've had a good marriage?"

"Ugh, well, I don't know anymore," Angela said truthfully. "I always thought we had a great marriage. Marcus has been my best friend. I always thought we could talk about anything, and we actually have fun together. Plus, we're the ones our friends come to for marriage advice."

"But what?"

"But here we are," Angela said, throwing up her hands at the obvious question. "I told Marcus that I'm willing to give us another try, but I'm still trying to process the fact that he cheated. Marcus says he loves me, but am I supposed to just accept that depression made him do it? I don't know if I can buy that. I keep thinking – oh, never mind."

"Please continue Angela," Dr. Rogers said. Marcus reached over and grabbed her hand, his eyes pleading her to keep talking.

"I just keep thinking that there must have been something wrong with us. Something wrong with me." The room grew silent as Angela paused to get her composure. Dr. Rogers handed her a tissue, then continued.

"Angela, do you believe Marcus loves you?"

Angela paused only momentarily then said, "That's the funny thing, Dr. Rogers. I honestly do. . . . I just don't understand how anyone who loves me could hurt me like this."

The room again went silent, and Marcus squirmed anxiously in his seat. The energy in the room quickly moved from reflective to tense. Dr. Rogers chose this moment to alter the direction of his questions.

"Marcus, I know you've started going to therapy to deal with your depression, right? Have you been able to examine any more about why you went outside the marriage?"

Angela noticed the way Dr. Rogers picked his words carefully, and appreciated his consideration. Since Marcus got out of the hospital, it had been difficult, even after she decided to try to work things out. Every time they seemed to put a piece of their marriage back together, the infidelity would resurface. Sometimes Angela brought it up to let him know she'd forgiven him, but not forgotten. Other times, Marcus would remember something else that he needed to be honest about, and that would start another discussion. It was as if all of his skeletons kept coming to the surface one by one, and he was trying his best to purge so they'd have a clean slate. It wasn't easy. In fact, they hadn't even made love since the first night he'd come home from the hospital.

Realizing he had yet to answer the question, Angela looked at Marcus expectantly. No matter how many times they talked about it, Marcus hadn't been able to explain it in a way that made Angela feel any better.

Marcus had told her how much he wanted to build something different from what he'd experienced growing up. He never wanted his kids to know what it was like to feel unloved and unsupported, and to go without the material things that other kids always seemed to have aplenty. He'd thought he had the perfect plan.

But, somewhere along the way the path had become less clear. The young boy with visions of a mega-empire looked up one day and suddenly realized he'd somehow turned into a man over thirty, stuck in a corporate job working for the man. He had no empire of any size in the making, and worse, the more he thought about kids, the more terrified Marcus became about not knowing how to be a good father. After all, he'd never really seen it done up close and personal. That's when he panicked and told Angela he didn't know if they would make it. The counseling back then had helped some, as had his move out of the corporate world, but none of it had made him feel whole.

After what seemed like forever, Marcus finally spoke up to answer Dr. Rogers' question about why he cheated.

"I don't know why I did what I did. I know I have trust issues. And I know that I have support issues. But I can't really explain. . . . I mean, I love Angie, and I've never loved any woman the way that I love her. But sometimes it just got to be too much."

"What do you mean?" asked Dr. Rogers.

Marcus shrugged his shoulders as if he hoped the doctor wouldn't push further.

"Marcus, if these sessions are going to be helpful, you've got to help Angela understand what you're thinking."

"I'm trying, I really am," Marcus began. "I just don't know how to put it into words. It's like sometimes I just felt like something was missing. And it just seemed like no matter how hard I tried, I just couldn't quite get there. Does that make sense?"

Marcus turned to speak directly to her. "But no matter what, you have to know it wasn't you." Marcus' eyes watered as he looked at her earnestly.

Angela tried to absorb his words and the emotion behind them.

"Angela can you accept what Marcus is telling you?" Dr. Rogers asked.

After hesitating momentarily, Angela finally said, "I'm willing to try."

"Well, I'd say that's a very positive place," Dr. Rogers said. "I'm glad you recognize that these things take time."

Dr. Rogers asked them a few more questions about the past, then gave them some exercises for home, one of which was to go out on a date.

"Marcus, I recommend that you try to focus on your individual sessions for the next several weeks, then I'd like to see you both back here ready to dig in more."

They couldn't have picked a more beautiful day to play hooky and have a picnic in the park. Though it was October, two full months since the hospitalization, the weather was mild even for Atlanta. It was as if God wanted to give them a little taste of Spring to help them make it through the brutal winter that was coming or to make up for the brutal season they'd already had.

"How's this for a spot?" Marcus asked, as he spread their blanket out under a tree.

"That's cool," Angela replied while unpacking their subway sandwiches and making herself comfortable.

Then seemingly as an afterthought, she asked somewhat casually, "What are you thinking about?"

"Huh? Oh, nothing really. Just enjoying the weather," Marcus said, as he stretched out on the blanket.

As he did so, Angela observed her handsome husband and wondered if anyone would ever guess by looking at them what they'd been going through. Having lost at least 15 pounds since his admission to the hospital, Marcus looked much like the college boy she'd met a decade before. He looked the same, he spoke much the same, and yet he was different.

He was quieter, slower, and all around more guarded than the man she once knew. Unlike her overly-sociable husband, this one was more of a loner and thought more; joked less. Which, of course, meant that she thought more too. Most of the time when they were together, she was observing and analyzing for anything out of the ordinary. She watched the way he took in their surroundings at times, and it made her think the remnants of paranoia were still present. Even during their down time, she couldn't completely relax for wondering what he might be thinking. Like now. As he looked around the park and appeared to take in their environment, Angela involuntarily found herself comparing his actions to Marcus of the olden days. *Was he just taking in the scenery, or more?* If he talked, Angela analyzed each word for any undertones. If he was quiet, she was constantly nagging him with "what are you thinking?" She didn't want to be overprotective, yet she didn't know how else to look for warning signs. The signs she now realized she missed before.

Angela was sure that her 'what are you thinking' question was only slightly less irritating than her other all-time favorite question, "have you taken your medicine?" As far as she knew had taken his medicine every single day since getting out of the hospital, and yet she just couldn't give it a rest. What was she so afraid of? It's not like he was really crazy. He's just been really stressed, that's all.

Relax in the moment, she told herself. *Stop over-analyzing.*

Angela lay back on the blanket and placed her head on Marcus' shoulder. Instead of focusing on the things that weren't the same, she made a vow to instead focus on the blessings. Marcus was much stronger than when he first came out of the hospital. He drove and went places alone, and though he wasn't taking on any real client work, he was slowly getting back into the fold. He'd gone to a business conference the week before and started to reestablish business ties. He'd even gotten active in her church and joined the choir. He knew he couldn't hold a tune, but said he enjoyed it, so she supported him. Best of all, they talked and shared intimate moments in a new way and really talked about the root of their issues in marital counseling. Maybe it's true that what doesn't kill you makes you stronger. Maybe their marriage would one day be a ministry of some sort after all.

Angela closed her eyes, inhaled the moment of peace, and held onto it for as long as she could. No sooner had she found that place where her mind was quiet, than he spoke.

"Angie, I've been talking to some of the brothers at the church about faith."

"Ugh-hunh. What about it?" She really wasn't in the mood for a deep religious discussion, but tried to go with it.

"Well, the Bible says that with faith, anything is possible, right?"

"Ugh-hunh."

"So, why are we so hung up on this medicine? Shouldn't I have faith in my healing? It seems like taking medicine says that I don't have faith."

Angela's eyes flew open. She'd wanted to know what he'd been thinking and there it was. She unconsciously held her breath for several seconds before she realized what she was doing.

"It's just that I'm tired of feeling half drunk or like I should be riding the short bus. Tired of popping pills all the time, and even more tired of you questioning me as if I'll come unglued if I miss one."

"What?" Angela bolted upright as if she'd been stung. "Sweetie, taking medicine doesn't mean you don't have faith. That's why God gave us doctors and medicine."

"Calm down, Angie," he said. "I'm not saying that I don't have things to deal with. That's why I'm going to counseling, so I can learn not to stress so much, and cope with the real issues. But, medicine doesn't help you do that. It's just a cover."

Angela placed her hand on his and looked him squarely in the eye. "Sweetie, you promised me and the doctor that you'd give it six months. Please, don't break this promise."

She hoped that he could read the not so subtle implication there. You've broken enough promises. Don't break another one.

Angela debated launching into another soliloquy about how sick he'd been and how scared she was when he was in the hospital. But, she could tell from his body language that he probably wouldn't receive it well. A look she couldn't quite decipher passed through his face before he spoke.

"Ok, Angie, I'll stick with the medicine. Now, let's talk about something else. . . . Let's just enjoy our day."

Angela wished she could erase the past few minutes and find the peace she'd glimpsed. Unfortunately, the moment had passed and her mind was back at work again.

25

"ANGELA, WE'RE GOING TO BE LATE. COME ON." Marcus yelled from the front room.

"I'm almost ready," she yelled back, though she knew good and well that it would be at least another 15 minutes before she was dressed and ready to leave for work. It almost felt like their normal routine from before.

Almost.

"An-ge-la!" he yelled again. "It's 8:30. Come on."

Since when have I ever gotten to work on time, Angela thought to herself as she stepped into some black high heel pumps. Then, grabbing her purse, she rushed to the front door where Marcus stood waiting.

As he opened the door to let her pass through, it dawned on Angela that she'd almost forgotten something important. If they had any chance at making it, they had to do this right. No shortcuts.

"Marcus, sweetie," she almost sang out, "we almost forgot your medicine."

"Oh, I can take it when I get back," he replied casually.

Angela's heartbeat increased just a tad, as she wondered what would happen if he didn't take the medicine. Although the doctor said the mere depression had caused the psychotic episode, he was clear that there was work to be done to find the underlying stressors so that it wouldn't happen again. Since their talk in the park a couple of weeks before, she'd been watching even more closely to ensure that he took the medicine every day.

"But, we have a routine, man!" she said, trying to make her voice sound light. "Come on, it's not like I'm ever on time anyway. I can wait."

Marcus knew her better than anyone else, and it didn't help that she was incapable of hiding her emotions. At that moment, he was looking into her almond-shaped eyes and likely seeing the fear that engulfed them. Lots and lots of fear. She held her breath subconsciously while waiting for a response.

The fear was well deserved. Even with medicine, he seemed frail. Although he didn't speak as if he were paranoid, she knew it still lingered by the way he'd checked the door before they went to sleep the night before. And the way he insisted that something was wrong with the light in the car, and took it apart to make sure it was working. Not to mention his lack of concentration. Here was a man who used to read a book in a day or two. Since coming home from the hospital he would sit with a book for hours, then complain that he had only made it through a few pages.

No, he definitely wasn't the man she'd married, but it was still way better than the one who thought folks were out to kill him. Angela would do anything to keep *him* from coming back.

"Marcus," she said, knowing that it wasn't *what* she said, but *how* she said it, that might express the importance.

"God, Angie, I was going to take the medicine later. But, if it makes you feel better for me to do it now, I will." he said. "Just don't let me hear one word about me making you late."

"You won't. I promise," Angela said.

"The things I do for you woman!" Marcus said, attempting to lighten the mood, and sounding like his old self.

With that, he went back into the kitchen and grabbed the prescription bottles from the bar, along with a water bottle. Meanwhile, Angela knew she was doing a horrible job of pretending not to watch, as she followed his each and every move.

He made it easy for her. One pill out of the bottle into an open hand. Into his mouth, followed by several long gulps. Second pill out of the bottle and into an open hand. Into his mouth, followed by several more long gulps.

For added affect, he ended with an "Ah-h-h."

And, they were off to another day.

"Angela Bennett," she said, picking up her office phone.

"Hey chica, did I catch you at a good time? I'm tired of talking to your voicemail at home and on your cell, so I decided to try you in the office. Can you talk?"

"Endi! Hey, girl! I'm sorry I haven't called you back the last few days. Just haven't been in a real phone mood." Angela got up to close the door so that her secretary and neighbors didn't overhear all of her business. Bad enough they knew something was going on.

"Yeah, well, I'm going to forgive you *this* time. But next time, not so much. Don't scare me like that! Shoot me an email or something to let me know you're good."

Though she knew Endia couldn't see it, Angela smiled at her through the phone.

"Ok, so spill. How are you?" That's Endi. Straight to the point.

"Well, things were going pretty well . . . ."

"And? What happened?"

"Well, it's probably nothing, but . . . well, a couple of weeks ago Marcus asked me if I believed that God could heal him without the medicine."

"What?"

"Yeah, it freaked me out for a minute that he was even thinking that, but it's probably nothing. . . . We talked about it, and he understands he needs to keep taking it and going to counseling. He promised he would, so it's ok."

Angela could envision Endia's smirk, then softening of her features as she chose a less direct response. "Angie, if you're so convinced that it's nothing, why is it bothering you?"

Checkmate. Angela hated when she did this. It was bothering her because those little pills were the difference between a man who Angela could talk to and a man who thought she was plotting to kill him. It bothered her because she just couldn't go through that again.

"It's not bothering me, so I don't even know why we're talking about it. . . . Anyway, let's talk about you."

"Ok, if that's what you want."

Grateful that Endia let her off the hook so easily, Angela realized that there are times when true friends look the other way when you lie. It's not that they don't know; it's that they realize you're not ready to admit the truth, even to yourself.

Why is it bothering me? Angela kept thinking later that day as she opened the door and stepped into her home. Immediately all thoughts of medicine and worries about Marcus ceased, as she took in the family room.

Candles were lit along the fireplace, window sills, and table, giving the room a beautiful glow. The aroma from the kitchen made Angela's stomach growl and reminded her that she hadn't eaten all day.

"Hey, baby, I didn't even hear you come in," Marcus said, coming up to give her a small peck on the lips. "Go get comfortable. . . . By the time you come back, dinner will be ready."

"Wha? . . . . Marcus, what's all this?"

"Hmm, let's see . . . . It's called taking care of your wife for a change."

"But, what made you do all this? I mean, I . . ."

"Angela, stop," he said gently. "Stop thinking and just relax. Don't think, just enjoy it, ok?"

Marcus was right. Angela's mind had been thinking and rethinking on all of the what ifs that could happen instead of just being in the moment. As she slipped out of her work clothes and into her standard boxers and t-shirt, Angela decided to just let go. Tomorrow would take care of tomorrow, so for now, she was just going to be grateful for today.

Marcus was chopping tomatoes for the salad when she walked up behind him in the kitchen. Angela put her arms around his waist and hugged him from behind, just as she'd done a hundred times before, but not since the hospital.

"That feels nice," he said, putting the knife down to squeeze her hands.

Relaxing into the moment in full, Angela stood on her tiptoes and kissed the back of his neck. Then, squeezing him tighter, she slowly left a trail of soft kisses down the side of his neck. Marcus mumbled something unintelligible in response, then turned around to face her. Their eyes locked and Angela felt her pulse quicken in the way it used to – before.

Marcus caressed her cheek, then mimicked her earlier kisses by making a trail down the side of her neck, as his hands caressed her body softly. Though her eyes were closed, she sensed his lips coming towards hers before she tasted their sweetness. They fell into the familiar, not stopping for air; not even stopping as the oven timer started to beep.

Angela had the sensation of falling, yet she wasn't afraid. Because this time, Marcus was there to catch her.

26

"**A**NGELA?"

Mary's voice sounds so far away that it takes me a minute to realize she is actually calling my name. I open my eyes, somehow surprised that I am still in her office.

"An-ge-la, you with me?"

I pull myself back to the present and nod my head in response. Looking around the room, I see that Mary has kicked off her shoes and tucked her feet beneath her. I sit up and rub my eyes, adjusting again to the fluorescent overhead light.

"Can I have another water?" I ask, then laugh when Mary points to the bottle in front of me. I assume she placed it on the table while I was talking, but I didn't even notice.

"Angie, I know it's going to take time to fully explore everything, and we can't do it all in one session, but since we're nearing the end of our time for today, it might be helpful for us to clarify your goals for our time together. Would you say that you're here to finish healing from the infidelity? Or perhaps from your husband's hospitalization?"

It's my turn to draw my knees in to my body and begin rocking. Only when I am safely in fetus position do I dare look at Mary.

"I'm here because I keep trying to figure out the lesson in all of this and figure out what I'm supposed to do next. My

147

mother would say that it's to build my faith, but I just don't get it. This isn't how things were supposed to be."

"But I thought you said things were going well, and you two were rebuilding your marriage? Has something changed?"

I close my eyes again because I don't want to see the look in Mary's eyes when I respond.

"Yes. . . . Everything."

27

"HEY YOU," ANGELA SAID, AFTER PICKING UP HER office phone. "I'm glad you called. I was wondering how your research was going today."

She smiled, thinking about how proud she was that Marcus was back working. She'd seen the draft of a website he was putting together and had to admit that it was the best he'd ever done. It had been almost three months since the hospitalization, and with each passing day he'd seemed to gain more energy and to be happier all around. Maybe he'd finally adjusted to the medicine.

"What's taking you so long?" Marcus asked.

"What do you mean? So long for what?"

"So long to get downstairs," he said, sounding like he was trying not to grow impatient, but not winning the battle.

"Marcus, it's 4:15. Why would I be ready to leave this early? Besides, I thought you were working late today to finish up your website."

"Didn't you tell me to come around 4:00?"

"Huh? No . . . In fact, I told you this morning that I might need to stay late. Don't you remember? . . . If you needed to leave the city early, you should have told me and I would have driven my car."

"No, that's no problem. I just wrapped up early because this afternoon I heard a voice that sounded like yours, telling me to come early. 'Be here around 4:00,' it said. I could have sworn that it was you."

Angela tried to stop her heartbeat from increasing, thinking there must be a rational explanation for what he'd said. *A voice like hers?*

"Angela, are you still there?"

It took a few seconds for her to speak, but she finally mumbled what she hoped was an intelligible response.

"Sweetie, you thought I called you today?" she asked, then closed her eyes to pray as hard as she could that he said yes.

"No, not on the phone, Angie . . . Anyway, don't worry about it. Do you want me to come back later?"

She didn't respond. She couldn't respond. It was happening again.

"Angie?"

"No . . . Stay there . . . I'll be right down."

Angela tried to center herself as she hung up the phone. *Breathe. Just take a moment to breathe and do not panic. One breath at a time. Do not panic.* She continued the effort while gathering her purse and the file she was working on. There must be a logical explanation.

Soon she was exiting the building through its revolving doors. Right away, Angela spotted their SUV along the curb a few cars down. She tried to make her lips curve upward into a grin, but the action felt forced and unnatural, as if she hadn't truly smiled in ages. So instead, Angela focused on walking forward instead of doing what she wanted to do – which was to run quickly in the opposite direction as if none of this was real.

As she got into the car, they exchanged niceties and Marcus began the drive home in rush-hour traffic. For the first fifteen minutes, Angela prayed for the right words, the right questions, and for peace – no matter what. Finally, she spoke.

"Marcus, what did you mean when you said that you thought you heard my voice today?"

"Just what I said."

"Could you explain to me how you'd hear my voice if I didn't call you?"

"I'm still working on that. I don't really understand it. Sometimes I hear these voices, but I haven't quite figured it all out yet."

Angela's heartbeat increased so much that it felt as if her heart might come out of her chest at any moment. She had to stifle the urge to ask Marcus to let her out of the truck right then.

What in the world did it mean that he was hearing voices?

"So, you hear voices of people who you can't see?" She tried to make her voice sound as casual as possible, but the last words cracked as she stifled a sob.

"Sometimes," he said, sounding bored.

"When did this start?"

"Um . . . let's see . . . it started in the hospital, but it stopped for a while and started back again a few days ago . . . Hey, do you want me to stop at the Chinese place?"

How could he think of food? Didn't he realize how crazy this was?

"No, Marcus, I'm not hungry . . . Look, I have to ask, have you changed anything with your medicine?" Angela worked to keep her voice calm, although inside she was on the verge of falling apart. She kept thinking the answer had to be no, because she'd seen him take it every single day. Hadn't she?

"You know how I feel about medicine. I stopped taking it last week, but I didn't tell you because I didn't want to have this conversation we're having right now. I'm not even going to talk about it . . . If you're sure you don't want Chinese, I'm going to drive on home. Ok?"

Angela didn't even know if she said anything out loud in response. How could she think about food when her husband was hearing voices? Clearly that meant he was experiencing some sort of psychosis, but did this also indicate that his problem was more than depression? Could the doctor make him take the medicine so the voices would go away? It had crossed her mind that Marcus might go back to the paranoid state he was in before, but never had she considered the possibility of him getting worse.

She had to call Dr. Alexander.

An hour later, after three pages to the doctor, the Bennett house phone finally rang. Seeing "Peachtree Hospital" on the caller id, Angela pressed "talk" on the cordless receiver and walked into the guest room. She shut the door behind her and hoped that Marcus couldn't hear.

"Hello," she whispered.

"This is Dr. Alexander."

"Yes, Dr. Alexander, this is Angela Bennett. I've been calling about my husband."

"Yes, Angela, how are you?"

"Marcus stopped his medicine. I guess he's been pretending to take it. . . . And, today he told me that he's been hearing voices."

"Oh, that's unfortunate," he said calmly.

"Unfortunate? What exactly does that mean?" Angela tried to be cool, and to keep her tone low, but could feel an edge creeping into her voice.

"Well, voices are typically evidence of some sort of psychotic break. Not taking the medicine obviously allowed the symptoms to return and possibly even worsen – assuming that he's never heard voices before."

"What?" Angela was about to lose it. "Look, Dr. Alexander, Marcus was getting better. He was doing well – I mean, at least he wasn't having psychotic episodes that I know of. Now we're back to square one. No, worse than square one. Please, you've got to help us." Finally, the tears began to fall.

"I'm sorry, Mrs. Bennett. I know it must be difficult, but Marcus has got to take responsibility for himself. You can't make him do anything as long as he's not a danger to anyone . . ."

"I'm tired of hearing that same old line about him not being a danger to anyone. You can't believe that Marcus is capable of making an informed decision when we now know he's interacting with people who aren't there? I mean, what are we trying to protect? His right to be crazy?" Angela realized that some of her frustration was misplaced, but she couldn't help it. "I know that if Marcus was thinking clearly, he would never choose this for himself. He wouldn't want to be this way! There just has to be something you can do . . ."

There was an awkward pause. Finally, Dr. Alexander spoke in a more compassionate tone, probably realizing that he had two crazy patients on his hand.

"Tell you what, Angela. If he's willing to talk to me, I can try to get him back on the medicine, but I'm not optimistic about him listening to me. Most times, folks have to hit rock bottom before they admit to needing help."

At least Dr. Alexander's proposed course of action was less drastic than mixing medicine in Marcus' morning juice, which was what Angela was considering.

"Yes, please. Let me see if I can get him on the phone."

Angela hurriedly ran to the front room and told Marcus that Dr. Alexander wanted to speak to him. To her surprise, Marcus shrugged his shoulders and followed her back toward the office. She prayed, while simultaneously putting the phone in the office on speaker.

"This is Marcus."

"Hello, Marcus. I'm just checking in on you. Your wife sounds concerned."

"Ok."

"Well, she tells me that you've heard some voices. Is that true?"

"Yes."

"Well, I'm a little concerned about what that means. I know you talked about not wanting to take medicine, but I think the voices could indicate some of the issues we talked about before. I know you don't want to go back to where we started in the hospital."

"I appreciate your calling, but I'm fine."

"Well, maybe you should come in so we can talk —"

"Like I said, I'm fine. . . I'll talk to you another time."

With that, Marcus hung up the phone. He then went to take a shower in the master bathroom without seeming to notice that Angela was crying softly at the office doorway.

28

ANGELA WASN'T SURE HOW SHE MADE IT THROUGH the night, let alone dragged herself into the office the next morning. All she knew was that she dare not stop, because if she paused to really process it all, she probably wouldn't ever get back going again.

Just as Angela got settled in her office, the phone rang. Glancing at the caller ID, she saw the name Naomi Peterson.

How long could she avoid her calls before Naomi demanded a real explanation? Angela felt guilty for not being able to talk straight to her best in-town friend, but it was just too complicated. For one, Naomi was a licensed psychologist, which meant she would want to review Marcus' situation, then counsel Angela on what she was feeling. No way she was ready for that.

Plus, though Naomi's husband, Micah, and Marcus weren't real close, they'd considered doing some business together, and all of the circles were just too small for comfort. If Angela told Naomi what was going on, Naomi would likely tell the other part of their threesome, Deb. If Naomi told Deb, Deb would probably tell her good friend, LaTonya. And so on and so on and so on. Even though they'd all be well-meaning, everyone would have their advice on what Angela should do. Worse yet, there would always be that look in their eyes as they talked about "poor Angela." No way she was starting that wildfire.

Angela waited for the phone to go to voicemail so she could listen to the message, then respond by email or by phone at a time when she was sure Naomi wouldn't be in. Instead, to her dismay, Angela heard the phone stop ringing and the light next to line 1 grow steady – an indication that Trixie had picked up her line.

Thirty seconds later, Trixie came to the door.

"Angie, Naomi is holding for you."

"Thanks, Trixie, but could you please take a message? Tell her I'm tied up."

"Oh, I'm sorry Angie. I already told her you were here because she was rather persistent with her questions about what you were doing . . . It will probably sound strange if I try to backtrack now. I knew she was a friend, so I said more than normal. I'm sorry if I shouldn't have."

Angela sighed and tried to think of how to get out of talking to Naomi, but quickly concluded that there was no way around it.

"Ok, put her back through," Angela said, without even attempting to hide her frustration. "After this, please just let all my calls go to voicemail."

"Whatever you say," Trixie replied, clearly confused by her Angela's tone. Leaving the office, she closed the door behind her. Moments later, the phone buzzed to signal that Trixie had forwarded the call to Angela.

"This is Angela."

"Ok, so is it something I did, or did you just wake up one day and decide you didn't like me anymore?"

"Naomi . . . no, of course it's nothing like that . . . You know how it is sometimes when you start running in a bunch of different directions. Between work and home and everything . . . It's just been crazy." Now that was the truth. Loosely.

"Girl, I have been calling you for almost three months! Three months! And the only reason I didn't just camp out at your office or on your doorstep is because I get these pitiful little emails or voice messages every blue moon that let me know you're still alive."

"Yeah, well, you know how it is," Angela repeated, because she couldn't figure out what else to say.

"Well, this morning I realized how long it's been, and started thinking that for all I knew Marcus might have lost his natural mind and tied you up in the closet or something. That's what you've driven me to. I haven't been able to get a live person for so long that my mind has started playing tricks on me. Frankly, I didn't know what to think. This is so unlike you. Are you ok?"

"Yeah . . . I'm fine."

"And?"

"And . . . um . . . I'm sorry," Angela offered, realizing even as the words came out how flat her response sounded. Unfortunately, though, her emotions only worked in an on or off setting these days, and there was no in between. If Angela turned "on," she might never regain her composure.

"Sorry? Angela, is that really all you're going to say?"

She remained silent, unsure of what to do.

"So, you're not tied up? You're alive and healthy? You just haven't had time?"

"Well . . . yeah, I've just been really busy . . . You know how it is." Why couldn't she think of anything else to say? Ask her to understand? Tell her she wasn't ready to talk about it yet?

"Well, when I called you two weeks ago, it was to tell you that I'm pregnant. So there's my big news," Naomi told Angela with anger rising in her voice. "I thought that being my friend and all, you might want to share in what's going on with me . . . I guess you've got too much going on with work and home and *everything* to even care."

"Naomi, I . . ." Angela opened her mouth to say something – perhaps to confess in full – but stopped when she heard a click, and then dial tone in her ear.

Angela sent up a silent prayer of protection for Naomi, Micah, and the baby to come. Yet, Angela couldn't bring herself to call Naomi back.

Naomi and Angela met soon after Angela moved to Atlanta. Not only did they have lots in common, they discovered that they had gotten married within a month of each other. So they'd become fast couple-friends, and coincidentally, both couples had thrown out birth control around the same time. By all accounts, they should all be pregnant and happy right about now. The thought brought an uncharacteristic surge of jealousy, and Angela placed her head in her hands to pull herself together. She was truly happy for Naomi, but Naomi's happiness was like a mirror, forcing Angela to look at how crazy her own life was right now.

Before she could process it any further, her office line rang again with a number she didn't recognize. Angela hoped it was Naomi calling back. She'd have to find the words to tell her what was going on and to apologize.

"Angela Bennett."

"Angela, hey . . . It's Lela; Lela Mason. I hope you remember me. We were in that mediation course together last year." The voice sounded like that of a young girl, and wasn't one that Angela recognized.

It took a few moments for Angela to place the name, but then finally it clicked. Why had she answered a number she didn't recognize? Lela had seemed nice enough the few times they had met, but Angela didn't feel like casual banter. Especially with an almost stranger.

"Lela? Of course, I remember you . . . I'm kind of in the middle of a few things at work, but what can I do for you?"

"Well, I know we don't know each other that well, and I definitely don't mean to pry —"

Angela hoped she would get to the point soon.

"Look, I don't know how to say this nicely, so I'm just going to say it . . . And I'll try not to be too blunt . . . But first, are you ok? Derek and I have seen you at church a couple of times lately and . . . well . . . You look like hell."

Angela opened her mouth to say something back, but to her surprise, what came out was a loud, belly-wrenching laugh.

"Lela . . . oh my God . . . that was you not being blunt?" She could hear that Lela joined in laughing with her.

"Girl, I'm offended!" Lela said, feigning indignation. "That was me at my most sensitive!"

Wow, it felt so good to laugh. Funny how it's sometimes easier for a perfect stranger to give it to you straighter than your own friends can. Outside of the sketchy calls to her family, and the conversations with Endia and Christine, Angela hadn't really spoken to anyone about what was going on. Angela called Endia every time she needed advice, especially given that her friend had experience with mental-health issues. She called Christine every time she needed a shoulder to cry on, especially since that wasn't exactly Endia's strongest point. She was more of a tough-love friend, while Christine would hold her hand when Angela needed coddling.

Meanwhile, her Atlanta friends were all getting the same excuses about why she hadn't been around and no one in town who knew the truth. Angela wanted to protect Marcus' reputation so he could rebuild his business when he was ready. How would he ever do that if folks thought he was crazy? How would she ever live it down?

Though these thoughts went through her mind when Lela called, Angela's mouth was obviously on its own agenda. Apparently, some part of her knew that she needed to talk. So Angela did.

"Lela, I can't believe I'm even doing this, considering that we don't know each other that well, but do you still work a few buildings down from me? I could really use an ear — maybe we could get together after work one day?"

"Yeah, sure . . . And actually, I'll do one better. How about you meet me at the Starbuck's in fifteen minutes?"

"But it's two o'clock in the afternoon! I can't have you taking off from work! Aren't you still working in the district attorney's office?"

"Yep, I am. And the way I see it, the same criminals I could prosecute today will be the same criminals I can prosecute tomorrow . . . Besides, from the sound of your voice, you'd be better off billing the next hour to me anyway. Call it 'professional development.'"

Angela giggled at the notion of jumping ship. Not like she was getting anything done at work anyway.

"You know what, Lela? You're right. I'll see you in fifteen."

"Well, don't be late. The last one there has to buy the coffee."

"For real? Then I'm already at the elevator!"

As Angela rushed into the coffee shop, she was disappointed to see that Lela was already seated at one of the oversized chairs near the back. She got up and hugged Angela warmly before Angela took off her coat and sat down.

"Dang, girl! Judging from the looks of you, I'm almost feeling bad for making you pay," Lela said in the soft baby voice that Angela had learned was the real deal. If nothing else, that voice offered comic relief, because every time Lela spoke, Angela wanted to say, "Stop playing and talk like a grown-up." Especially after she also detected a slight lisp. It wasn't much of a match for the powerful attorney that she knew Lela to be. Lela's appearance didn't seem to fit, either, in that she was barely five feet tall. The other contradiction was her hair. This toffee-colored sister had shoulder-length hair that looked way too fine-textured to be her own, especially when compared with what Angela observed around Lela's hairline.

"What do you mean 'judging from the looks of me?'" Angela asked, as she looked down at what she liked to refer to as her law firm uniform. Today it was an Anne Klein gray pantsuit with a pink shirt that peeked through the slight opening of her jacket. Granted, her hair wasn't freshly cut, but it was pulled back neatly.

"Angie, it's not what you're wearing down there. It's what you've got going on all up and through here," Lela said, gesturing to Angela's face, and smiling at her sympathetically. "You look like you just saw a car wreck or something. What's going on?"

Angela's forced smile quickly dissolved as she realized that she couldn't pretend anymore. As Lela saw Angela's eyes become glossy, she reached over and grabbed her hand.

"Don't worry, Angie. I can't imagine anything you could tell me that would be bad enough for me to let you off from treating today. That's the kind of friend I am," Lela said, with a smirk that made Angela laugh and release a few tears, all at the same time.

"I can't believe I'm about to spill my guts to a stranger," Angela began, as Lela looked at her supportively. "Ok, well, here goes. In August, my husband had a nervous breakdown, checked himself into a mental hospital . . ." she said, then paused to sigh before continuing.

"Admitted to cheating with a bunch of women, convinced me not to divorce him on the spot, came home after only four days 'cause the doctors are just plain dumb, and now every day I try to convince myself that the worst is behind me while I'm living with a man that I don't even know and who I can only hope to trust. To make things worse, he decided to stop taking his medication. And yesterday he told me that he's been hearing voices." She paused for air while wondering what in the world this woman must think of her now.

Lela sat there with eyes protruding like golf balls, her hand across her mouth. Then, as Angela looked on in confusion, Lela stood up from the table.

"So you want grande or tall?"

That question made Angela smile through her tears.

"I'll take a chai tea latte with soy, please."

"Coming right up."

When Lela returned to the table several minutes later, she placed the cups on the table, then sat down and grabbed Angela's hand again.

"Angela, I can't even imagine what you're going through. Me and Derek have had our fair share of issues, but so far both of us are still hanging on to our faculties . . . I was joking about the coffee thing, but really, your story is worse than anything I could have imagined. I'm just in awe that you're holding it together as well as you are. What happens now? Did the doctors say if he'll be ok?"

"They say yes. With counseling and medicine. But. . ." Angela paused as she decided to be brutally honest with Lela and herself.

"But, what?"

"But, deep down, I don't know." Angela bit her lip to keep from crying and glanced around to see if the women at the next table had heard any of their discussion, before deciding that it really didn't matter anyway.

"Have you tried getting his family involved? Or what about the church?"

"No, I haven't really talked to his mom yet, but that's a good idea. And, do you really think the church might help?"

"Doesn't hurt to try, right?"

Angela nodded.

"So, Angela, what can I do?" Lela squeezed her hand and looked at Angela warmly.

"Honestly, Lela, you've already done it." Angela placed her other hand on top of Lela's. "I didn't feel like I could talk to any of the folks who know Marcus. And I hadn't realized until you called how much I really needed someone to talk to.

"So, thank you. Thank you for noticing, and for caring enough to call."

29

WHEN 11 A.M. SERVICE ENDED AT CHURCH THE following Sunday, Marcus was ready to head to the car, but Angela stopped him.

"Marcus, I know what you said about the medicine," she began, "but how about we get some spiritual guidance from Pastor Murray?"

"Why?" he asked.

"Sweetie, stopping your medicine is a big decision. I really would feel better if we had her thoughts, since she's someone we trust. Would you please talk to her? . . . For me?"

Sighing, Marcus nodded his head slowly. "Fine."

"Excuse me," Angela said to an usher passing by. "How can we get in to see Pastor Murray?"

"You want an appointment with Pastor Murray? Well, I can give you the number to call the church secretary tomorrow, but she'll probably schedule you with one of the assistants."

"Assistant? Appointment? No, you don't understand. We really need to see Pastor Murray today, about . . . an urgent matter. And it's really time-sensitive."

"I understand, and I'm sorry, but Pastor Murray books appointments for weeks – sometimes months – in advance. You understand. Ministering to a congregation of this size keeps her pretty busy. But I'm sure one of the assistant pastors can help you."

Angela's eyes began to water again and she struggled to keep her voice steady. "Look, I hear you. And I appreciate what you're saying. But I'm telling you that we need to see her today. . . . Isn't that what the church is here for? To help people in need?" Her eyes pleaded with the usher to have a heart.

"Ok, baby, I'm sorry for whatever you're going through. I can see that you're having a hard time. Tell you what, give me your names then I'll personally go up and see if Pastor Murray is around. Ok? And if she's not here, then I'll make sure we get someone to pray with you before you leave. Ok?"

Angela just nodded her head and mumbled a thanks.

Twenty minutes later, the usher escorted them back to the waiting area outside of Pastor Murray's office. And forty-five minutes after that, Pastor Murray opened her door to invite them in. Angela and Marcus followed the clergywoman into the room.

"So, what brings you here today?" she asked, smiling broadly, after they had all taken a seat. Angela suddenly wished she'd been more than a pew warmer so that the pastor would know more about them than their names. If not for the limited interaction in new members' classes, she probably wouldn't recognize them at all.

"Pastor Murray, I have a question," Marcus said. "I was wondering . . . what does the Bible teach us about faith?"

Pastor Murray looked a little confused that faith was the reason for an emergency meeting, but recovered quickly.

"Wow, Marcus, I could preach a whole sermon on that question," she said smiling. "But for now, I'll just say that it's really simple. With faith, anything is possible."

"Really? . . . Anything?"

"That's right, anything. The Bible gives us great examples of faith making seemingly impossible things possible. People getting through impossible situations. People getting healed from seemingly incurable diseases. And the examples in the Bible are no different from what we can experience today."

"Thank you, Pastor Murray," Marcus said and smiled, then gave Angela a triumphant look. "I asked because my wife and I seem to disagree on what it means to have faith. I want to stop taking depression medication, because I really believe that God can heal what caused the depression – not medicine."

"Well, Marcus, that's true. God is in the healing business," the pastor said. "But sometimes he uses doctors too."

Angela gave Marcus a look that said "see, I told you," but he ignored her.

"I understand Pastor, but I don't like the idea of putting chemicals in my body that don't address the real problem."

"Well, Marcus, I can't give you medical advice, but I can tell you that I've had other members decide against taking antidepressants. It's something you need to be prayerful on because every situation is different."

"That's what I've been trying to tell Angela," he said smugly.

Pastor Murray just sat there smiling, as if her work was done. Angela decided she had to jump in, but carefully so as not to alienate her husband more.

"Pastor Murray, Marcus' depression was really severe. . . . It caused a lot of . . . issues." Angela struggled for the right words. "It was more than just simple depression. . . . I'm really afraid that if Marcus stops the medicine now, we'll lose the progress he's made."

Angela paused, then started again, "I just want my husband to understand that taking medicine doesn't mean that he lacks faith, because God can use the doctors and medicine to heal him."

Pastor Murray scrutinized Angela and Marcus closely, as if trying to read between the lines at what they weren't saying. "Oh yes, of course. I hope I didn't give you the wrong impression.

It's not necessary for you to do without medicine to show your faith. God knows your heart. And God surely can use the doctors to heal you."

"Thank you, Pastor Murray," Marcus said. "I understand."

"So will you start back taking the medicine?" Angela asked.

"No," he said, then stood to indicate that the meeting had come to an end.

"But Marcus, you promised you would do the meds and counseling for six months like the doctor recommended!"

"Look, I know what I promised, but this is one promise that you'll be glad I didn't keep. Just trust me," Marcus said.

With that, he walked quickly out of the office, not caring that he was leaving Angela and a very confused looking pastor behind.

"Lela, I am so sorry to just barge in on you like this," Angela said apologetically, as she walked into the foyer of her new friend's home later that afternoon.

"Girl, please," Lela said in the soft baby voice that still threw her for a loop. Lela hugged her tightly and showed her into the family room. Lela's tastes were quaint and simple, but the photos of her smiling two-year-old son brought warmth to every corner of the room. In fact, Derek Junior was the only one whose pictures were displayed. Not even a wedding photo captured the married couple.

"Well, I really appreciate you. One day when I'm normal again, I plan to show you that I'm really not a crazy, high-maintenance, energy-sucking drama queen."

They both chuckled together – Angela, because she realized that Lela probably didn't believe a word she said, and Lela, because she really didn't believe a word Angela said. Maybe there was some liberation in being crazy. It meant you could invite yourself over to a virtual stranger's house. That is, if you could even call them strangers now. In the few days they had been reacquainted, Lela had called Angela every morning and evening to make sure she was ok, and to pray with her. Maybe it was time to call her "friend."

"So how's it going today?"

"Worse," Angela said and filled Lela in on their disastrous meeting with the pastor. "I finally told him that if he didn't at least go see the doctor, I was moving into the guest room. Know what he said?"

Lela raised her eyebrows and asked, "do I even want to know?"

"Let's just say I'm staying in the guest room now. . . . It's just so crazy! It's like his emotions are gone. I can yell, cry, or scream and he doesn't even seem to notice. He barely even talks to me anymore and I just don't know what to do."

Lela shook her head and placed her hand over her mouth. "I'm so sorry. You always hear these stories of people having breakdowns –"

"But you never think it happens to normal people, right?" Angela's eyes flooded with tears. "I just don't know what to do."

"What does his family say?"

"Not a whole lot. Last time I called his mom, she said she'd try to get some time off work. I don't think she gets it."

"I think you should make her get it. She doesn't get to just check out. He's her responsibility too."

"Do you think I should try her again?"

"Yes! I would have her on automatic redial about now," Lela responded, then smiled. Angela noticed for the first time that she wore invisible braces. *Maybe that's where the lisp comes from.* "Derek isn't here, so we have the house all to ourselves, but you can use the phone in the guest room so you'll have privacy. It's the first door on the left down that hall."

"Thank you."

Fifteen minutes later, she came out to find Lela sitting on the couch in the family room. Emotionally spent, Angie sat down beside her without saying a word. She lay her head back and tried to quiet her mind.

"Well?" Lela prompted, after several minutes of silence.

"I'm all out of options. I just finished a very one-sided conversation with Marcus' mother."

"What do you mean 'one-sided'?"

"It means that I spent ten minutes trying to convince her that it's worth her time and money to come down here and see about her son. Then, when that failed, I offered to foot all the expenses for her to get here. When that failed, I just hung up."

"Girl, you hung up on your mother-in-law?" Lela laughed and looked at her in shock.

Angela couldn't help but laugh before responding. "I've never disrespected her. Not in ten years. And I didn't mean to do it this time. It's just that . . ."

"What?"

"Well, I'm just tired of doing this by myself. One of the reasons Marcus and I are in this space is that Marcus never felt supported when he was growing up. I'm not blaming his mom, but I'm mad that she's trying to make this just my problem. Ya know?"

"You're right. That's not the way it should be, but you know how older folks are. No telling what made her who she is, and it's probably not a good idea to expect her to change. You might just have to accept that she's who she is. Period."

"Yeah, I got it. I just don't know who else to call. Marcus is the oldest, so no way he'd listen to his younger brothers. He hasn't talked to any of his friends about this, so I don't want to get them involved. Plus, I doubt he'd listen to them anyway 'cause he's usually the one giving advice, not taking it . . . So what do I do?"

Lela didn't answer right away, but instead reached over and grabbed Angela's hand.

After a quiet moment, she gave Angela some familiar advice. "Well, I know this isn't easy, but my guess is that you just wait . . . and pray . . . and hope for the best."

30

No one would guess that it was Thanksgiving Day, given the activities in the Bennett household. Angela had woken up early – or rather she'd gotten up early since there was little or no actual sleep for her during the night. The mattress in the guest room wasn't great, and she wasn't used to sleeping by herself. Plus, she kept waking up whenever she heard any little sound. Finally, Angela had put a chair behind the door to make herself feel better. Though she didn't think Marcus was dangerous, she didn't want to take any chances on what one of those voices might tell him to do.

As soon as it was late enough, Angela called her family to wish them a Happy Turkey Day. Hopefully, they were fooled by the false lightness Angela tried to force into her voice as she quickly got on and off the phone. She didn't want them to worry unnecessarily.

Placing the phone back on its cradle, Angela quickly surveyed the guest room. That was where she'd been sleeping for the past few weeks, since Marcus' refusal to take the medicine. At the time, Angela had thought that the ultimatum might clue him in to how serious she was and force him into action. Instead, he'd carried on as if it were business as usual.

Just then, her cell phone rang. Seeing that it was Lela's number on the caller ID, she picked up quickly.

"Hey, girl," Angela answered.

"Happy Thanksgiving!" Lela greeted her joyfully.

"Same to you."

"Ungh-ungh, I don't like the way you sound."

"It's the same old, same old . . . I'm fine, really." Angela lay back in the bed and pulled the covers up under her chin.

"What happened?"

"What hasn't happened," Angela said, resigned to the fact that this was her new life. She ran her hand through her mess of uncombed hair and closed her eyes tightly.

"Spill."

"Let's see, where should I start? On Tuesday, I got a call from a partner who I used to work with at my first firm," Angela began. "After beating around the bush, he tells me that Marcus called him to ask for legal assistance. Seems he needs someone to find cases about people hearing voices."

"What?"

"Oh yeah, and it gets better . . . After that happened, I swallowed my pride and called Marcus' mother again to beg her to come help. Do you know what she had the nerve to say?"

"I'm afraid for you to tell me, but what?"

"His mother said that she *might* get some time off work next month! . . . And she wonders why her son is crazy? When she can't even make her way down here when he's sick? I even offered to pay for the ticket! Not that money is the point, because if it were my mother, she'd have sold barbecue dinners and Cool Cups to get here!"

"Girl, I'm sorry. That's just . . . beyond crazy."

"Tell me about it." As Angela turned over on her side, she caught a glimpse of herself in the floor-length mirror beside the bed. Her eyes were red-rimmed and swollen, and her face looked pale.

"Well look, I know this won't make things better, but what are you guys doing for dinner today?" Lela asked.

"Hmm. I'm thinking that it's going to be a tough choice between microwave popcorn and ramen noodles. Which do you recommend?" Angela laughed.

"Angie, you can't be serious! It's Thanksgiving."

"Yeah, well, I'm not feeling very thankful today."

"Well, I don't care. You and Marcus are coming over for dinner. I'm not taking no for an answer."

"Ok, so which part of 'my husband is crazy' did you miss? I can't bring Marcus to your house for dinner! Besides, he probably wouldn't come anyway. Plus, I'm a mess." Angela frowned as she sniffed under one of her armpits and realized that it was probably time for a fresh pair of pajamas. She hadn't gone into work Tuesday or Wednesday, and had basically been camped out in the room since then.

"I'm thinking that Marcus will come over if you tell him that Derek will be here. He's met Derek at the Men's Ministry meetings, so he might be cool with it. Either way, you need to get out of the house."

"I don't know if I feel up to it."

"Then I'll see you at around 2:00 . . . Bye."

"I don't . . ." Angela tried to respond, but Lela had already hung up the phone.

Surprisingly, Marcus didn't object to the idea of going to the Mason's house for Thanksgiving. He simply said ok when she asked, so Angela was hopeful that they could have a normal day. She managed to clean herself up a bit and threw on some leggings and a light sweater. They arrived at Lela's house just after 2:00 p.m.

"Hey, man! I've got the game on in the living room," Derek said, as they walked in.

"Cool . . . Let's do it." Marcus somehow managed to look excited, although Angela doubted he even knew whether it was football or basketball, let alone what teams were playing.

Grateful for the reprieve, Angela joined Lela in the kitchen. "What can I help with?"

"Girl, please. Rest yourself."

"Okey doke. You don't have to tell me twice," Angela said, while sitting down at the bar. Angela felt momentary embarrassment as she took in Lela's pretty sweater, skirt and boots – a great contrast to the outfit she'd pulled from the bottom of her closet. Angela had slicked her hair back and put on a little eyeliner to try to make her eyes look less haunted, but she wasn't sure it had done the trick.

"Lela, if I didn't say so before you hung up on me, thank you so much for inviting us. Marcus seems really comfortable, and I'm glad we didn't just let this day pass at home."

"No problem at all . . . I'm just going to get this last dish out of the oven and we'll be ready to eat."

Several moments later, Lela called everyone into the dining room and they all found a chair. Even Derek Junior sat at the large table with the help of a booster seat.

Once seated, Angela felt herself relax completely.

"Marcus, would you pass the green beans, please?" Lela asked, smiling at him.

Instead of responding, Marcus look disturbed, said "Excuse me," and got up from the table. He appeared to be heading for the guest bathroom down the hallway.

Angela focused so hard on her plate that she could swear her eyes should have left a mark on it. Then she began cutting her turkey into small, bite-sized pieces. When that task was done, she went to great lengths to butter her bread perfectly on both sides. Then she got some cranberry sauce – though she hated the taste of it – and began mixing it into her dressing. Maybe if she kept focusing on her food, the crazy man in the bathroom would evaporate, even if just for the day. Maybe for one hour she could pretend to be normal, like before.

"Angela, do you think you need to check on Marcus?" Lela asked, after at least fifteen minutes had passed. Then she diplomatically added, "Maybe he's not feeling well."

She wanted to say, "No!!! I don't want to check on him. I want to leave him here with you and Derek." Instead, she put on a neutral mask, nodded at Lela and Derek, and calmly got up and went to the bathroom door. All the way there she hoped and prayed all was well, but she knew in her gut that it wasn't.

"Marcus? Are you ok?" she inquired through the closed bathroom door.

"Is that you, Angie?" Marcus said, sounding distressed. "We need to leave now."

"What?" she asked, her voice rising. "We haven't even eaten yet."

"Angie, we need to go right now," he repeated while opening the bathroom door.

Angela didn't have the strength to argue or question. Instead, she just went back to give her apologies to their hosts.

"Marcus' . . . uh . . . stomach is upset. I'm afraid that we're going to have to go," Angie told the couple, though she figured everyone knew that it wasn't Marcus' stomach that wasn't well. "I'm sorry, Lela. I know how much trouble you went to for us."

"Are you sure?" Lela began, but stopped as Derek gave her a look that likely said, "Baby, let that crazy man get on up out of here."

"Well, let me at least wrap up some food for you," Lela said, rising from the table.

"Thanks, girl," Angela replied, though she knew in her heart that the food would likely be placed in the refrigerator to mold, like all the other food items she had placed in there since Marcus was hospitalized.

As they were leaving, Angela realized that with all the prep she did on her food at the table, she'd forgotten to bless it and tell God all the things for which she was thankful. Just as well, because she was beginning to feel like she didn't have anything left on that list.

As soon as they were out of the door, Marcus began talking to Angela excitedly as they walked toward the truck.

"Look Angie, I want you to check out this book I got from the bookstore on telepathy," he said eagerly. "I think it explains what's been happening to me. I've been reading it, and a few other books I've found while doing my research the past couple of weeks."

"What? You're kidding, right?" *Telepathy? He can't be serious.*

Immediately Marcus began to withdraw, as if he knew it had been a mistake to try to share. Angela hoped that every crease in her face said that she wasn't open to hearing him. She wanted Marcus to shut up and keep his craziness to himself. This was insane!

"Marcus, you seriously think that you're experiencing telepathy?" she asked dubiously. "Is this why you wanted to leave Thanksgiving dinner? Is this what you've been work-ing on during the day? I thought you were working on your business?"

"I am working. This is what I've been researching. I've learned so much already, but there's lots left to do if I want to get to the bottom of this."

"What are you talking about?" she asked, with a look that said "I've already decided that you're off your rocker, but I'm going to listen to see just how far."

Marcus looked at her as if she were the enemy.

"Look, Angela, I thought maybe you'd want to support me for once, but it's clear that's not the case." He opened the driver's door of the truck and climbed in, shutting the door loudly behind him.

Angela stood in the driveway of the Mason's home, fuming for a minute before she finally climbed into the passenger door of the truck. Once in, she turned sideways in the seat to look at him.

"Support you *for once*? Marcus, seriously, you do remember all the times I've had your back, even before now. Don't you?" Angela didn't know if she was more angry or frightened at his selective memory.

"Actually, no. What I remember is when I wanted to start my business instead of getting an internship, and you had the nerve to ask me about a business plan," he began, with his hand gesturing animatedly. "And when I wanted to buy some commercial property after we moved to Atlanta, you thought it was too risky. In fact, the more I think about it, the more I realize that you're the reason that I've never met my goals. I should be a millionaire by now, but you've held me back. You've never supported me or been there for me. Especially not now when it matters most. I should have never married you." Marcus looked at her angrily, then looked away in disgust as he started the car and backed out of the driveway.

"You can't be serious!" Angela yelled, still turned sideways in her seat and glaring at him in amazement. She touched his arm lightly and moved in closer. "Marcus, seriously. What about how I wrote half of your business school papers when you were tired, even though I was working crazy hours at the firm? Or how I came home and cooked almost every day because you were running so much with 'school' and I wanted to make sure you were taken care of?

"What about how I told you to quit your job to start your own business, even though you didn't even have a business plan finished and didn't have a real clue as to what you wanted to do – all because I supported your dreams? Even though I was just as miserable as you, working in a job that I absolutely hated!"

Angela continued to glare at him, as he kept his eyes focused on the road without even acknowledging that she had spoken. She felt her anger increase. How dare he just ignore her?

"Or, what about worrying over you every single second of the day – wondering if you're taking your medicine, if you're having paranoid thoughts, if you're going to be ok – all because I love you that much, but you don't think I've supported you?" Angela's face alternated between anger and hurt, but Marcus never noticed because his eyes didn't leave the road.

It was as if she'd never spoken. When Marcus finally began to talk, he just kept right on listing Angela's so-called short-comings without even acknowledging that she'd said anything. Angela watched the ranting of the man she didn't know anymore and sighed inwardly.

Maybe if she were less supportive, she'd actually have the strength to leave.

31

A SMALL MOVEMENT CAUGHT MY ATTENTION AND pulled me back to the present. It was Mary, trying to discreetly grab a tissue for herself. She dabbed quickly at the corner of her eyes before recommending that we take a short break.

I took my time finding the bathroom around the corner from Mary's office, hoping to give her a moment to regain her composure. I'd never have expected a counselor to become emotional – weren't they supposed to have heard it all?

Back in the office several minutes later, I sat quietly on the love seat, waiting for her to take the lead.

"I'm sorry about that," Mary said, giving me a tentative smile. "As a counselor, my job is to listen and to help you find the answers to your questions. But, from time to time, something hits a little close to home."

I wait for her to say more, but she doesn't. Instead, we sit there for a few seconds in an awkward silence, with me unsure of what to do or say.

I sense that it is my turn to listen, so I say nothing, even as the silence lingers. Mary looks like she isn't sure if or how to proceed, but finally she begins to speak, so softly that I find myself holding my breath to ensure I don't miss anything.

"I had a brother," she starts, then stops to sip her water. She doesn't cry, but the shake of her voice gives away her emotions.

"We called him Junior, but his real name was Bill.

"Bill was about three years older than me, and I loved him in the way that little girls love their big brothers. We fought all the time, but if anyone even looked at me sideways, Bill would handle it. So, I guess you could say that I knew he loved me too." Mary smiled, obviously lost in thought.

"He had this personality that I can't even begin to describe. That same kind of magnetic personality that you talked about with Marcus. Everybody loved him; he was one of those people that never met a stranger.

"Anyway, when Bill was about 19, something changed. Out of the blue, he seemed to turn into a completely different person. He was moody and aloof. Stopped hanging with his friends. Sometimes he'd say mean things to me for no reason at all.

"Finally, he started talking more and more about people that were out to get him. It scared me when he talked like that. But, quite honestly, we didn't really know what to do. My parents thought it was a teenage phase that he'd grow out of. He didn't. And, eventually, he was diagnosed as schizophrenic."

My heart does a quick shuffle at the mention of the mental illness. I don't like the subtle comparison that what she's been through is like what I've experienced with Marcus, but I feel her pain nonetheless.

"Anyway, I won't bore you with all of the details," Mary says, likely sensing that I have had about all I can take of her story. "I just thought you'd want to know that I feel what you've been through."

We both sit there with eyes glazed over, clearly no longer caring about the counselor-patient boundaries. If nothing else, we share something more, that others could try, but likely never quite understand. What it's like to see someone you love going through something, and to feel so incredibly helpless.

"I'm really sorry for what you went through with your brother." I finally say.

"And I'm sorry for what you've gone through with Marcus. I have a little sense of how it feels, and know it's not easy to see someone slip away."

There is that comparison again. I don't like where this is headed.

"Mary, just to be clear, with Marcus it's different. His doctor only diagnosed him with depression."

The silence that follows is uncomfortable, but I wait patiently for her response.

"Angela," she starts, back in what I presume is her soothing counselor voice. "Obviously I haven't seen Marcus, and don't know what he's going through. It's just that the type of experience you describe is typically life altering. It takes a bit of work to get a full diagnosis, but the symptoms you've described typically are more than depression."

I shake my head to dismiss the notion that Marcus is mentally ill or schizophrenic. Her brother is different from Marcus, and it was wrong of her to compare them.

Marcus is different, right?

32

I'VE GOT TO GET UP. ANGELA WILLED HER EYES TO OPEN AS the alarm clock continued to beep. She'd already pressed snooze three times, so being late was a foregone conclusion. Only the fear of what they'd do if she got fired was enough to finally spring her into action.

When Angela finally managed to peel her eyes open and literally crawl out of bed, she made her way to the master bedroom closet to find something to wear. Unfortunately, like everything else, the dry cleaning had slipped to the back burner. Her suits all needed to be cleaned, and lay in a heap at the back of the closet. Angela shamelessly went through the pile, trying to see if any one of them could be resurrected with a little Febreze and iron action, but those bad boys were beyond done.

Finally, in an act of desperation, Angela pulled out an old cream skirt-suit that used to be her favorite for interviewing back in law school days. It was still in plastic from the cleaners, in the place where she put things that she pretended not to want to wear anymore. Angela thought that with the right undergarments, she just might be able to pray herself into it, despite the twelve or so pounds gained after law school.

The suit didn't fit very well. In fact, it didn't fit at all. But instead of being too small, it hung as if it were at least a size too big. Angela stared in the mirror in amazement, as if someone had done the okey doke and switched her clothes for someone else's. Curious, she tried on another old suit to find that it was also too big.

Angela figured it shouldn't have come as a big surprise that she'd lost weight. She'd spent most of her time trying to make sure Marcus was ok. Before he'd gotten too paranoid to eat her food – a wise move on his part – she even cooked for him sometimes without eating herself. She just didn't have much of an appetite. Angela never imagined, though, that she'd lost that much weight.

Need to lose weight? Find out your husband is crazy and cheating. Instant appetite suppressant.

On her way out to work, Angela thought, just for old times' sake, she'd try again to encourage Marcus to go to the doctor. After all, any day now he might come around. Right?

"Baby, I'm leaving," she said, poking her head into the office where Marcus sat at the computer.

"Ok," he replied, without looking away from the screen.

"I know we've talked about this before . . ." Angela paused to gather her thoughts, then continued. "But I just thought I'd see if maybe you'd given any more thought to . . ."

"Angie, I don't want to talk about that again."

"But sweetie, I just thought maybe you prayed about it some more, and maybe . . ."

"Angela, I'm not going to keep having this discussion with you. I don't need to go to the doctor 'cause I'm not depressed," Marcus said, his brows creased. "But if you're so anxious to make someone crazy, why don't you look at yourself?"

"What? What do you mean by that?"

"You don't eat," he said, turning to look at her for the first time. "You cry all the time . . . You don't want to go to work . . . Humph, I think you're the one who's depressed." Marcus ended his statement with a hearty laugh as he got up and walked out of the room.

Angela stood there in shock.

As crazy as it was to take advice from the emotionally impaired, for once Angela thought he just might have a point. She could feel herself slipping away and losing touch with all the things that mattered. Maybe she did need help.

Angela didn't know why it was so hard for folks – especially black folks – to admit when they needed someone to help work through things. Why was there such a belief that they had to be so strong, or that asking for help was a sign of not having faith? Angela was beginning to think that sometimes strong is stupid, and that faith without works just isn't faith at all.

Since she was already late, Angela went back into the guest room and combed through her wallet for the little card with information on her employee assistance program. The one she'd tucked away without thinking she would ever have to use it.

When she didn't immediately see the card, Angela was tempted to put her purse away, climb back into bed, and call in to work. Again. It took every bit of her strength to keep looking, finally find the card, and then call the number.

"Hello? Yes, I'm calling because I'd like an appointment with a counselor, please."

"What's your name, social security number, and who is your employer?"

Angela provided all the information, then waited expectantly to get the time and place of her appointment.

"Ok, Ms. Bennett, do you have a pen and paper?"

"Uh, yeah, but for what?"

"Well, I'm going to give you the name and phone numbers of a few counselors who might be able to see you."

"Oh, I can't just make an appointment through you?"

"No, ma'am. That's not the way this works. I just provide you with some options. Once you speak with the counselors that I provide, if they don't work out, you can call me back and I'll give you more choices."

"Oh . . . Ok . . . I just thought it would be easier."

Angela jotted down the names and numbers, then set out to make the calls.

Three calls later, Angela had made an appointment for late January with one counselor, and had scheduled for early February with another. Both promised to call her if there were any last-minute cancellations before then. The other counselor wasn't accepting any new patients.

Maybe she could hold on till January. Then again, who was she kidding? Only a very thin thread was holding Angela from going completely over the edge, if she hadn't gone already.

Once in the office, instead of dwelling on her own emotional issues, Angela tried her best to focus on work. She was doing a pretty good job of getting part of a brief written, until the ringing phone interrupted her. It was an external, unknown number. She started not to answer, but feared it might be something having to do with Marcus.

"Angela Bennett," she answered curtly.

"Hey, Angie. Long time no hear from . . . It's John." John Jackson was an old friend from law school who touched base every now and again to make sure all was well.

"John, it's great to hear from you," Angela responded, hoping she did a better job at faking enthusiasm than it sounded to her ears. Nothing personal, but she just wasn't feeling very sociable these days. Angela tried to think quickly about how she could get off the phone without sounding suspicious.

"Look Angie, I'm not going to hold you. But I got the strangest email today."

Could she claim a work emergency? Say she needed to run to a meeting?

Angela held her breath at what was coming next, wondering if Marcus had contacted him for legal assistance.

"Oh really?"

"Yeah . . . well . . . actually, the email was just a sentence or two from Marcus, asking that folks check out his new website. Once I took a look at it . . . Well, I just wanted to make sure you'd seen it."

"Uh . . . Thanks, John," she said, trying to sound neutral. Angela jotted down the Web address and wondered if she could fake a bad connection to get off the phone.

"Look, John, I have another call coming in, but I appreciate your call. Take care." She hung up while he was still talking.

Angela's hands trembled as she typed in the Web address on her computer. Could it be different from the website she saw a few weeks ago that Marcus was working on?

As the page came up, Angela relaxed a bit when she saw how nice it looked. Using Flash technology that she didn't even realize Marcus knew, he'd incorporated nice graphics and video clips in a way that only a true technology wiz could pull off. Pure genius, considering he had no formal computer training.

After the Flash graphics intro, the first page of the website appeared. It included a plea for contributions to an organization geared to thwarting injustices. Ok, so far it looked pretty normal, although Angela had no idea what injustices Marcus was fighting against.

Reading a little more, it became apparent why John called her. Angela struggled to hold it together as she read that the main injustice was Marcus' coercion into the mental hospital where he'd been "forced to endure electromagnetic/microwave therapy."

As if that weren't bad enough, the next link she clicked on was a blog about Marcus' life. In journal format, he'd included a detailed account of events from the time he was hospitalized. As Angela read about the day that Marcus came to her job (with Angela's full name and firm name given) and about the day he told her about his infidelity, she felt physically ill. No more secrets. They all knew everything. Friends and co-workers now knew her every little secret in vivid detail. Raised to believe that you keep your dirty laundry to yourself, Angela found these revelations to be more than she could take. But what could she do?

Before Angela could read any more pages on the site, her office phone rang again and she saw the name Naomi Peterson on the caller ID. After debating momentarily, Angela picked up the phone.

"This is Angela."

"Angela . . . My God! Are you ok? I just got this email from Marcus and I went to the website and . . . Oh my God! I don't even know what to say . . . I am so sorry . . . I'm . . . I'm just speechless."

"It's ok . . . I should have told you, but I just . . . I just couldn't."

"No, it's my fault. Normally, I would have known something was wrong . . . Would have been more sensitive . . . It's these darn hormones, I'm convinced. They've just got me completely thrown off. Then I threw my pregnancy at you . . . I just feel horrible."

"Naomi, really, truly it's ok. You know I'm happy for you. It's just . . . weird timing is all. We were supposed to get pregnant together." Angela realized that the last part of her sentence may not have even been coherent because she started sobbing somewhere in the middle.

"Angie, are you ok? . . . Man, I'm all the way in Woodstock for a doctor's appointment, but I can be there in an hour. We can go get dinner or something. Or you can come over . . . Just tell me what you need and I'm there."

Angela smiled through her tears, wondering what took her so long to talk honestly with her friend.

"No, no, girl, I sound worse than I am. Really. I've got work to finish, and I'm really tired . . . I know you want to be there for me, but I just can't talk about it yet. Can you just be patient with me a little longer?"

"Of course . . . I just want you to know that I'm here when you're ready. Day or night, just call."

"I know. And I appreciate you."

"Ok . . . Well, you call us anytime. And I'm going to keep checking on you."

"Thanks, Nay,'" Angela said. Then as an afterthought, she added, "And congratulations. You're going to make a wonderful mother."

After Angela hung up the phone, she packed up her briefcase and left the office, not even looking back as she heard her line ringing again.

On the drive home from work, Angela tried to figure out her next move. She considered putting medicine in his juice, but realized he probably wouldn't drink anything she gave him. Besides, one dose might not be enough to make a difference.

Next, she thought about lying to say that he was dangerous. If it worked, they'd have to hold him for three days . . . But if it didn't work, she would be toast. And if Marcus was still mad when he got out, she would be triple toast.

Still contemplating what to do next, Angela was lost in thought as she walked into the house.

"Hey, Marcus," she said absentmindedly.

"Hey." After his greeting, Marcus began mumbling to himself. Angela wanted to ask her husband who he was talking to, but then thought better of it.

Walking back to the guest room, she stepped out of her shoes and pulled out her pajamas, though it was only five. But as she did so, a thought crossed her mind.

What was Marcus working on? He was so engrossed in labeling packages of some sort that he barely looked up when she came in.

Walking back into the family room, Angela approached the table and peered over Marcus' shoulder where several spiral-bound documents lay in front of him. She could almost make out the handwritten title on the front.

Just a little bit closer and she could read it.

Angela rubbed her eyes, convinced that she couldn't have read what she thought she read. She looked down again and saw it clearly.

Angela's Journal.

Moving to the other side of the table, still certain that she must have read it wrong, Angela picked up one of the booklets and read it again. *Angela's Journal.*

As she leafed through the pages, Angela felt something snap inside of her. All of her thoughts – personal thoughts from her journal that had been meant for only her and God, that she had been recording for the past four years – had been copied and bound into booklets. There had to be at least ten copies on the table.

"Marcus, what . . . are you doing . . . with my journal?" Angela was so intent on trying not to yell that she feared he may not have heard her. "Marcus? Did you hear me?" She tried to turn up her volume slightly without going into crazy-girl mode, which was about a millisecond away.

"I didn't think you'd mind," he said calmly. "I needed more evidence for my case against the hospital." Marcus resumed labeling envelopes as she stood there trying to will her brain to function.

"Who . . . are . . . you . . . sending . . . *my* journal to?" She willed herself to take a deep breath and not scream.

"Well, I have a list of key folks." Angela wouldn't have guessed that his voice could get even calmer than before, but it did. Without staying focused, Angela might soon believe that she was overreacting, given his extreme calmness.

"Like who? Who could possibly need to see this?"

"Here, take a look . . . I've got a few representatives and senators, Al Sharpton, and the President."

"The president of what?" she asked, her voice cracking.

Marcus' dimple deepened as he smirked at her. "Of the United States, silly."

Angela wasn't sure how long she stood there trying to figure out how to rationally argue in an irrational situation. Obviously, the "Fool, people don't mail personal journals to the President" was not the best approach, since Marcus couldn't see it on his own. How could she get through to him?

"Marcus, I want to help you, but there's a lot of stuff in my journals that has nothing to do with your hospital stay. I'm just not comfortable with that. Isn't there another way for you to prove your case?"

"Uh, well, I don't know. This is really important."

Angela tried to think of ways she could convince him to willingly return her private writings. Then she got an idea.

"Marcus, what if I just give you the pages about the hospital? Would that be ok?"

"Ok," he said, without emotion and while continuing to label envelopes.

Still dazed, she ripped out the pages about his hospital stay, then gathered the full journals to take to her room. It took her two trips to complete the transfer. Then Angela walked quickly into the guest room and shut the door wondering what in the world to do now.

That night, Angela went into the walk-in closet of their master bedroom. It was the only place she could think of where she could have at least an illusion of privacy in the house, since Marcus was "working" in his office. She wanted to place another urgent call to Marcus' mom. Angela didn't even wait for Regina to say hello. She just jumped right in.

"Please come and help him," she whispered. "He needs you, and I need you too. We can't do this alone. Someone has got to talk him into getting help! Please!"

As with the first call, Angela heard a long dramatic pause.

"Look, if money is the issue, I'll work it out," Angela added. "If I need to buy the plane ticket, I'll do it. And if your job is an issue, we'll make sure your bills get paid. We just need help." Heck, Angela would have begged, borrowed, or maybe even stolen to get Regina there.

After another long pause, Marcus' mom finally responded softly. "Well, it's just that he probably won't listen to me, ya know?" Regina spoke in a timid voice that Angela had never heard her use. Clearing her throat and steadying her voice, she continued. "He's always been so independent. Even as a child. I just don't think me coming down there would make a difference."

Angela wanted to scream, but didn't. That would take more energy than she could muster. So she just quietly hung up the phone without even waiting for Regina to say good-bye.

Her mind was consumed with all the things she'd tried that didn't work, then replaced with the sheer embarrassment that everyone knew. He'd told her co-workers, friends, and all the folks who used to think they had a great marriage. They all knew that he wasn't well, and that their whole marriage was a lie. Or, maybe they knew before Angela did. Maybe they had been whispering about her all along and thinking "poor Angela." How could she ever face them again?

On the other hand, she made a vow to love in sickness and in health. If she left, who would take care of him? Who would make sure he didn't hurt himself or someone else? How could she live with herself if he ended up out on the street somewhere – a homeless man talking to himself and asking for change on the corner?

Angela couldn't leave, but she couldn't stay.

What were the other options?

33

CAN'T DO THIS ANYMORE. **THAT'S THE THOUGHT THAT KEPT** rolling through Angela's mind the next morning, as she knelt beside the king-sized sleigh bed in their master bedroom. She'd gotten down on her knees to pray, then found herself inexplicably stuck. She just wanted this to be over.

Tears flowed uncontrollably from her eyes, as she rocked back and forth, in a way that rivaled Sofia in *The Color Purple*. It was the weirdest sensation. She knew where she was, and was aware of her surroundings, yet she felt completely removed. As if she'd entered into a space and time where it was just her and God. *I just want this to be over,* she thought again, praying that God could hear her thoughts and just open the bedroom floor and take her in.

Between the hysterical crying and talking to God, Angela heard a sound in the distance, a muffled voice that seemed to be getting closer. Some part of her brain realized that it was Marcus, talking to her. His breath tickled her eardrum, yet it felt as if he were miles away. Much too far for her to reach.

"Angela, what's wrong? Angela, why won't you answer me? Angela?"

Angela willed her mouth to respond, but what came out was probably unintelligible. She heard fragments of words "can't . . . do . . . this" and realized she wasn't making any sense.

Then there were more movements in the bedroom. The sound of something shuffling. What was he doing? Finally, she recognized the sound of a dial tone, then heard three beeps. "What's your emergency? Police, fire, or medical?" a voice asked over the speaker of his cellphone.

In a moment of coherency, Angela realized he was calling 911. The last thing she needed was for the police to come.

"Hang up," Angela said, finally finding her voice, although she had yet to open her eyes. "I'm ok." She wasn't sure at first if her words had come out clearly, but breathed a sigh of relief when she heard Marcus hang up the phone.

"Angela, what's going on? Angela!"

Aware that she couldn't stay on the floor and that God wasn't about to magically pull her up to heaven, Angela realized she needed a plan. Somewhere to go away from the madness that had become her life. Somewhere that didn't have crazy cheating husbands, bills, or jobs.

"Call my employee assistance program," Angela finally mumbled to Marcus, proud that she'd come up with something and formed the words to communicate it. Somehow, through the fog covering her brain, she managed to tell him where to find the phone number, then listened while he dialed the number.

"My wife is crying and won't get up off the floor," Angela heard him say in a dry tone, before handing her the phone.

"Hello," Angela said, her words likely jumbled among fresh sobs. "I need – I need to check in to a hospital." Angela envisioned the white, padded walls, medication, and even a strait-jacket like she'd seen in the movies; these images offered some weird sense of security and comfort. She wouldn't have to think. She wouldn't have to make any decisions. No one could bother her. No job. No responsibilities. No bills to pay. She could give in to the madness. No more pretending that everything was just fine. No more smiling on the outside when she was crying on the inside. It felt almost as good as the thought of death. Angela breathed a deep sigh of relief.

The counselor asked her a series of questions, most of them to ensure that Angela wasn't in any immediate harm from someone else. The last question she heard was "Are you suicidal?"

Angela tried to process the question. Saying yes would mean defying everything that she was taught to believe, and yet if she were honest, death was exactly what she wanted. She would have paid someone any amount to give her an end to the pain. How could she convey this to the stranger on the line? This was her last chance.

"I wouldn't kill myself because of my religious beliefs, but I just don't want to go on," Angela finally said. Angela lay back with her hand over her eyes, and breathed another deep sigh of relief. Her tears slowed for an instant – the first pause in an hour or more.

"Ok, Ms. Bennett. We can get you in for an appointment on Monday."

Monday? Angela felt like the tiny fragments that remained were shattering.

Moments later, the doorbell rang, and in walked a police officer who had come in response to the call to 911. She gave Marcus a sympathetic look as she observed Angela laying on the floor.

"But I'm not the crazy one!" Angela wanted to scream, "It's him! It's my husband who belongs in the crazy hospital!" But if she did, she'd surely be taken to the nuthouse and locked up for good. Not the psychiatric hospital with the nice clean sheets and the group therapy sessions. The one that people never returned from.

These words formed in her mind, then froze quickly on the tip of her tongue as her eyes grazed Marcus' form. Looking at him, no one would believe that he was the real crazy one, and that he had driven Angela to this state. She almost laughed out loud, but thought better of it. For had she laughed, Angela would no doubt have sounded like she'd truly gone over the edge.

Had she?

Summoning strength from a reserve she didn't know existed, Angela crawled up from her cowardly position.

"I'm ok now," she told the officer. Then, speaking into the phone, Angela told the counselor, "I'll just call back next week for an appointment," even while knowing she wouldn't be calling back anytime soon. The image of Marcus signing her into a facility was enough to get her moving again, at least long enough to find some real help.

The counselor, sounding happy to be done with another file, gave Angela the number to call for an appointment and hung up quickly. The officer gave Marcus one last sympathetic look, then headed for the door. "Such a shame that he has to live with that," Angela could hear him think. As Marcus trailed the officer to the front door of their home, Angela closed the bedroom door behind her. She then took the cordless phone into the walk-in closet where she hoped to have some privacy.

"Mary?" Angela said, feeling weird to be using the informal first name she'd heard on the outgoing message. "This is, um . . . Angela Bennett. I don't know if you remember me. . . . I, uh, got your name from my EAP a while back and you said your next appointment was at the end of January . . ."

Angela paused to try to stifle the sobs so she could complete the voice message, then added ". . . but I really need your help."

Embarrassed by her outburst, Angela tried to regain her professional tone. "Sorry, um, yes, so if you would please call me when you have an opening. Thank you."

Something had to give today. This time Angela had gotten up, but next time she might not be so strong.

34

"SO THAT'S WHAT LED YOU TO CALL ME?" MARY shakes her head, likely still taking it all in. "My God, you have been through more than I can imagine. I knew your voicemail sounded urgent — which is why I scheduled you on my day off."

"Yea. I know I must have sounded crazy when I called you. I just didn't know what else to do." I pause to brush a tear from my cheek with the back of my hand. "I keep wondering, did I not pray enough? What did I do wrong?"

Mary stops taking notes and looks me squarely in the eye before responding, "What makes you think you did something wrong? Just because things didn't turn out the way you planned?"

"Well . . . yeah . . ." I take a tissue from a box to my right and consider the question for a moment.

"No one's life is perfect, Angela. We all go through stuff," Mary says, as she hands me another Kleenex and pats my hand before sitting back in her seat. "The important thing is that we go *through*, and we always get to the other side."

I sit there with tears flowing freely as I think about how much pain I've felt in trying to hold it all together. I am just so tired.

"Angela, it's obvious that you really love your husband. And I admire you for wanting to help get him through this. But, don't you think it's time to think about yourself? To protect yourself?"

"What do you mean?" I ask, as I feel my defenses rising.

"Well, you can start with little things like getting your own bank account to make sure you're not financially impacted."

My own bank account?

"You should also think about whether you're safe living with him. Has anything caused you to feel like you're in danger?" My head snaps up at the mere suggestion.

"Marcus would never hurt me," I say. "I know him."

I don't dare admit that I've been sleeping with a chair behind my door because I'm scared of what the voices might tell him to do.

"Angela, I'm sorry to say this, but the man you knew doesn't exist anymore. The sooner you accept that, the sooner you can begin to decide what that means for you."

"Doesn't exist? What does that mean? How can he just be gone?"

"As I said earlier, it's true that some psychotic behavior can be seen in severe depressive episodes," Mary says, her face expressing empathy and concern. "However, it's more often seen in patients who are bipolar or schizophrenic. I just think that you should prepare yourself, because what you've described sounds like it is likely something more than depression."

My heart begins to race, as my mind continues to resist.

"But he's going to be ok. I just need to get him back in to the doctor. . . . It's like what my mom heard in her dream," I say, less confidently than intended. I have to say these words, if nothing else, to convince myself that I believe them.

We sit there in silence for a few moments, as I think about how I can make her understand. Mary gives me a comforting smile and leans in toward me.

"Angela, you're not responsible for Marcus," she says. "Even though he's ill, Marcus is still responsible for himself. And ultimately, only God can take care of him. You can stay in that house and drive yourself crazy if it makes you feel better. But at some point, you have to concede that God is the only one who can watch over and protect your husband. Not you. Not even his family. You've got to stop thinking that the answer lies with any one of you. Until Marcus is willing to admit that he needs help, there's nothing you can do."

I sit perfectly still and speechless, contemplating her words. But no matter how I analyze it, I can't imagine giving up on Marcus or on our marriage. How could I leave him when I promised in sickness and health, until death do us part?

"I thought my vows meant that no matter what, we're supposed to stay together until we die. Isn't that what 'til death do us part means? If not, what's the point of marriage? If people just bail when things get tough, why even bother?"

"So you think that people should stay together no matter what? Is that what you're saying?"

I hesitate then say, "I think so. Isn't that what God intended?"

"So, if a close friend came to you and told you that her husband was beating her – actually, let's make it even worse: her husband is beating her almost daily. She's tried to talk him into counseling. She's tried talking to her pastor. She's prayed. She's done everything she can think of to help her husband and to save her marriage. But, nothing has worked. What should she do?"

I smile a bit and shake my head, "Of course, I'm gonna say that she should leave him. No woman should stay in a situation that's abusive."

"Why?"

"Why? Are you kidding? Because no one deserves that. God wouldn't want her killing herself to save him. That's not what love is."

"Are you sure?"

I open my mouth to speak, then realize the corner I painted myself into. "But, wait, physical abuse – that's completely different. Marcus has never been physically abusive. He never even came close to hitting me. In fact, the worst argument we had ever didn't even include cursing."

"So, being physically abused is different from being mentally abused?"

"No, I'm not saying that. Mental abuse can be grounds for leaving too."

"Why?"

"Oh, here we go again. Because it's unhealthy. . . . Because —"

"Go ahead."

"No one should stay in a situation that's abusive, physically or mentally. Mary, of course I get that. But, I don't think I could characterize what Marcus has done as abuse."

"Angela, just because it's not intentional doesn't mean that it's not abuse. Just because he's not intending to hurt you, doesn't make the situation any less hurtful."

I am silent in response.

"Now, I can't tell you what to do about your marriage, but I can tell you this: no one should stay in a situation that's abusive."

Mary pauses to let those words sink in.

"So, Angela, if you decide at any point that the relationship you're in is abusive to you; whether or not Marcus intends it to be, you don't have to stay."

"You don't have to stay," she says again for emphasis.

"But —"

"Angela, you don't have to make any decisions today. Just promise me you'll at least think about it? Also, please think about coming back to see me?"

I close my eyes and pray for strength, then slowly nod my head. Seeing that my time has ended, I give Mary a quick hug, grab my coat and purse, and head out the door; back home to figure out what comes next.

PART III

"Putting Them Back Together Again"

35

IT WAS SO EASY FOR ME TO SAY THAT NO ONE SHOULD STAY where they are being abused, yet it is almost impossible for me to admit that this applies to me. I can't just throw out my marriage, can I? Not without doing everything in my power to make it work, right?

But what else is there left to do? I've tried time and time again to get Marcus back to the doctor, and to convince him that something is wrong. In the two weeks since my appointment, I've even tried to get him to go see Mary with me, but he's not trying to hear it.

I've repeatedly begged his family to help me get him back into treatment and keep getting the same lame excuses from his mom. Unfortunately, there's no one else to call.

I've prayed the same prayer so many times that I feel like even God must be saying "give it a rest, I heard you already." I've even wished that if God had to take someone, that he'd taken me. But it's as if God has turned a deaf ear.

None of it has brought Marcus back to me in his right mind. And none of it has given me peace, as I lay awake night after night, listening for any sound to indicate that one of the voices has told Marcus to push through the chair that still serves as a make-shift lock behind my door.

You can't stay here.

I don't know if it's God's voice or my own, or if they are one and the same. All I know is that this is the voice that I've come to recognize as my intuition. It's neither a scream nor a whisper; instead it's the epitome of peace and clarity.

You have to leave now.

I can tell by the calmness in my spirit that it is the right thing to do. Some part of me has known it since my session with Mary, but I just wasn't ready. I know that I need to go someplace, even if just temporarily, to regain my strength and peace.

Though I have yet to come up with a plan, I decide to do what I know is right. I get up and swiftly move out of the guest room into the home office where Marcus is sitting at the computer with his back to the door. He is typing furiously.

"Marcus?"

He keeps typing, as if he doesn't hear me, but I know he must because I am only a few feet away.

"I was thinking that it might be a good idea if I go stay with a friend for a while . . . That way we can have a little space. What do you think?"

I wait for some reaction, but he doesn't say a word and doesn't even turn around.

"Marcus, did you hear me?"

"I think that's a great idea Angela," he says, without breaking stride. "Now I can really devote my time to the foundation and my lawsuit." Nothing in his tone indicates that he is even remotely concerned.

I stand in the office doorway, wondering what, if anything, there is left to say; baffled that my intentions haven't even caused the tiniest of reactions on his part. He hasn't asked where I am going or if I am coming back. There is no sign that he cares at all.

"It's not like this marriage is gonna work anyway," Marcus adds, as he turns slightly in the chair to look at me. "So, yeah, you should go. Now."

Marcus starts to turn back to the computer as I stand there feeling dismissed. How dare he just blow me off like this isn't a big deal?

In that instant, my peace dissipates and for the first time, I feel angry. I want him to look at me, to acknowledge the pain I'm feeling and to at least pretend to care.

Before I can stop myself, I take off my two-carat, princess-cut diamond ring and throw it at him, as hard as I can. In my vision, it plops him upside his head and either knocks some sense back into him or gives him something to remember me by. Unfortunately, in reality, the ring swerves a little to the right, where Marcus catches it with ease. He shakes his head and smirks, as if belittling my outburst, then quickly puts the wedding ring into his pocket.

"Thanks. This will help with some of my legal fees," he says, then walks out of the room.

So much for that brilliant plan.

I'm not sure how long I stand there in a daze before regaining the ability to center myself. When I finally do, I pick up the phone to call Lela.

"Hey, girl," I say.

"Hey, you sound like crap. What's going on?"

"I just snapped," I say. "It's not worth going into the details, but it ended with me throwing my ring at Marcus."

"What? You did what?" Lela's baby voice rises an octave.

"Yeah, I just lost it."

"Ok, so can you just help me understand why when you 'lost it' you didn't throw a bowl or a vase like a normal person? What woman throws back her wedding ring?"

"Girl, you're crazier than I am." I try to laugh, but it comes out as more of a snort. There's nothing really funny about anything that just happened.

"Call me crazy if you want to, but Derek always knows what's up. I think your husband should be just a teeny-weeny bit scared of what you might do if provoked." Lela says in a convincing voice. "Anyway, enough on that. Tomorrow we'll figure out where Marcus stashed the ring, but tonight you sound like you need an escape. Want to come over for a while?"

"Uh . . . Well, actually that's an understatement . . . I want to come over for a long while . . . Lela, I don't even know if I can ask this . . . ."

"It's done," Lela says, before I can even put my request into words.

"What? What's done?"

"You need a place to stay and we just so happen to have room at the inn . . . So it's done."

"Girl, I —"

"Angie, I know we haven't known each other long, but just please come get the key," Lela says in a tone that indicates that the subject is no longer up for debate.

"But I'm not even packed . . . It'll probably be the weekend before I —"

"No, come get the key today," Lela insists. "I know you. You wouldn't ask unless it was really bad. And, all jokes aside, for you to be throwing stuff means you're on the edge. Whether you come today or next week is up to you, but I want you to have this key so that you know you have someplace to go whenever you're ready. If nothing else, that will make me feel better . . . ok?"

I try to swallow my tears as I thank my new friend and hang up the phone.

One step forward, but towards what?

36

IT HAS BEEN TWO WEEKS SINCE I MOVED IN WITH LELA and I still don't have a plan. I look around her guest room, observing the floral and paisley prints, from the bedspread to the throw-blanket on the wooden rocking chair. Nothing in this room tells me what I should do next, if anything. I just want to stay here hidden away from the world.

In the time that I've been here, things have gotten worse, which is funny because I didn't realize I had yet to hit rock bottom. Christmas has come and gone, and I've had very little contact with Marcus. When I call he either ignores the phone, or talks quickly because he thinks there are people listening. He won't turn on the television because he thinks there are people watching. He spends all his time on so-called research of what the hospital has done to him. I never want to go back, and yet, I don't know how I can stay away.

A knock on the door interrupts my thoughts.

"Come in," I say, not even bothering to get out of bed to open the door.

Lela pokes her head in first, as if to see if the coast is clear, then pushes the door open wider so that she can enter the room. Finally spotting me, hidden away under the covers, she comes over and sits on the edge of the bed at my feet.

"Hey . . . I was just coming to check on you . . . Haven't seen you all day."

I pull the covers down to my waist and slowly sit up in the bed. Rubbing my eyes, I attempt to smile at Lela's mother hen routine.

"I'm fine . . . It's just a day that I wish I could erase from the calendar."

"Well, you don't look fine," Lela says, likely taking in my swollen eyes and uncombed hair. "What's the significance of today?"

"December 30th . . . was the day we got married . . . Five years ago. It doesn't even seem real now."

Lela's face apologizes before she finds the right words to match her sentiment.

"Sweetie, I'm sorry . . . I had no idea . . . Five years, huh?"

"Yeah . . . I was just sitting here wondering if I'm supposed to be celebrating, mourning, or just ignoring today altogether . . . We had such a beautiful wedding. A huge wedding party. All my friends and family. The works."

Lela pats my leg and waits for me to continue.

"I just thought it would turn out differently, ya know? . . . It may sound cliché to say it, but for as long as I can remember, I've known what my life would be like. After college, I'd get married to Marcus. We'd have two or three chocolate bundles of joy, and though I figured we'd have problems just like everyone else, I just thought it would be stuff like – I don't know – fighting over bills or something. Never in a million years could I have imagined that I'd move out because my husband wouldn't take medicine for whatever was going on with him mentally. I thought by now I'd be all swollen up pregnant somewhere. Instead, the only doctor's visit I need is. . ." I pause and look away, regretting that it almost slipped out.

"Angie, what were you about to say?"

"I really don't want to talk about it. I didn't mean to even go there . . . Everything is fine."

"Angie, what were you about to say? Could you be pregnant? I know you said that you and Marcus slept together a couple of times after you got home . . . Is that what has you so spaced out today? If you're pregnant, we've got to get you eating and taking care of yourself better."

Lela's eyes look like they are about ready to pop out of her head.

"Lela, relax. I'm not pregnant."

"Are you sure?"

"Yes, Lela, I'm positive. I'm not pregnant. Not even possibly pregnant."

Lela exhales a little too loudly. "Well . . . then . . . what do you need the doctor for?"

I close my eyes, then blurt it out. "I need an HIV test."

Every sound in the room is suddenly amplified as I wait for Lela to respond. The clock on the wall, the toilet running in the adjoining bath, and even my own heartbeat fill the silent space.

I decide to speak first. "Marcus said he practiced safe sex, and he even got an HIV test while he was in the hospital. Yet the truth is, I don't know what he did and when the last time was that he did it. So I've been thinking that I won't know for sure until I take a test."

Lela pauses only momentarily before responding. "Ok . . . well . . . looks like tomorrow we'll be late for work."

"What are you talking about?"

"I'm talking about you and me taking the morning off to get you tested. They probably close early for New Year's Eve so we should go first thing."

"Lela, I don't know if I'm ready for that . . . And I can't have you taking off from work to hold my hand."

"Angela." Lela speaks my name as if it is a complete statement. "There comes a time in life when you have to stand up and fight. Now maybe you don't win in the way you expected.

Maybe you and Marcus don't get to live happily ever after. Still you have to stand up and face the fact that life just didn't turn out the way you thought.

"And you recalibrate. And you make a new plan. And a new life. In the end, you live happily ever after – maybe not in the way you thought you would, but happy, nonetheless. Tomorrow we're going to get you an HIV test, and then there'll be one less thing hanging over your head, so that you can be free to find your new plan. Ok?"

I hope Lela can see the slight nod of my head, as I cover my face and have one last cry.

37

I^{T IS EASY FOR ME TO PLAY THE ROLE OF VICTIM AS I} read the posters on the wall at the clinic. Despite my best efforts to look the other way, the brochure titles leap out: *What You Don't Know About Chlamydia. Everything You Need to Know About STDs.* Finally, *AIDS and You.*

It just isn't fair for me to have to be here, worried about diseases, when I was the faithful one. I wait for the familiar sensation of my eyes watering and my face flushing, but instead I just lay on the exam table feeling empty.

My thoughts are interrupted when the door to the exam room opens. In steps a middle-aged black woman with a short natural hairdo and no-nonsense posture. She dispenses with the formalities quickly and doesn't even look at me directly before getting down to business.

"Put your feet in the stirrups, please."

I do as I am told, though reluctantly.

"Now just relax."

I have never understood how anyone who knows what's about to happen can even pretend to relax. It's like saying, "I'm about to cut you, but I want you to just sit here and smile pretty for the camera." Like that makes any sense.

For a while, the doctor pokes and prods with her fingers as well as with instruments that I swear only a dungeon master could have made back in the fourteenth century, and then finally she looks at me for the first time. I can only imagine what I look like lying there. Though my hair has grown out of its style in the past few months, my wash and curl have done wonders to make me look and feel more human than I have in a while. Unfortunately, though, my eyes betray me. They hold memories of the prior months in a way that take away my youthful innocence, and make me look as if I've been through something.

As we've obviously passed the point of introductions, I take a deep breath and jump right in. "I'd also like an HIV test, please."

Slight wince, but no other discernible reaction. *Shuffle, shuffle, shuffle*, to get the right equipment to draw blood and forms. *Shuffle, shuffle, shuffle*, through what I assume to be routine questions.

"Are you married?"

"Yes."

"For how long?"

"Five years."

"Oh . . . And have you had any other sexual partners in the past several years?"

"No." I pause and search my brain for the right words. Best to just be anonymous — that's part of why I went to a clinic for a full physical instead of to my normal physician. But I still have to be truthful. Even after all I've been through, it is still hard not to play "perfect."

"My husband cheated."

First strong discernible reaction: Pity. She tries to cover it quickly with a professional, masked demeanor – the same mask she wore while probing and prodding my body. But I see the crack in her surface and it makes me angry. I don't want to be pitied. In fact, I don't want to be here at all. Certainly don't want this to be my life. I still am not convinced it is.

"Well, you'll want to have another test at least six months out from the last . . . um . . . encounter."

"I understand."

The last time I had an HIV test was when Marcus and I got engaged. Back then, I had been confident that, unless they weren't telling folks everything about how one catches the disease, I should be home free. Marcus was the second man I ever slept with, so as far as risk went, there seemed to be very little.

When I got my last HIV test, I felt so very liberated knowing that I was getting married and taking leave of the scary, disease-infested dating pool. No longer would I have to worry about things like sexually transmitted diseases, including AIDS. I was safe forever.

Maybe that is part of why I am so incredibly frustrated to be here. My safe haven was just an illusion . . . a mirage. While I was "forsaking all others," he was partaking in as many others as he wanted and exposing me to risks without remorse.

What will I do if I am HIV positive? I was so judgmental before, so quick to feel pity for others without ever really stopping to think it could happen to me. How strong will I be if I am one of "them?" I pray Marcus was telling the truth about using condoms.

"The results will be back in three days," the doctor says. "You have to come back in person for them. Also, before you go, one of our counselors will talk to you about the test, just to make sure you have all the information you need."

I nod my head and prepare to get down from the table and re-dress.

Fortunately, the talk with the counselor doesn't take much time. So before long, Lela is dropping me off at the firm with a hug and promise that everything will be fine.

Upon entering my office at work, I am overwhelmed by a blizzard of papers. Spilling out of my in-box. Stacked in seemingly chaotic heaps on my desk. Then my secretary brings in more documents from the mailroom.

"Mostly junk, but here's a personal one," Trixie says, handing me a large envelope before leaving the office and closing the door behind her.

"Marcus Bennett," the return address reads. I stare at the name for ten minutes before I finally get up the nerve to open the package. In fact, I am so rattled that I can barely manage the clasp on the envelope. My hand is trembling and I am scared about the possibility of tearing whatever is inside.

How can things possibly get worse?

38

MARCUS BENNETT V. ANGELA BENNETT, ET AL.
My heartbeat increases as I realize that this might be a divorce summons. I try to decide if I'll be sad or relieved if he has taken steps to leave me.

But, wait, as I read more, there are three other names listed as defendants. Reading more closely, I see my name is listed as a defendant in a lawsuit, along with the mental hospital and several other names I don't recognize. Stunned, I begin to read through the thirty-three-page document. My heart seems to have lodged in my throat as I realize that Marcus is suing me for placing him in a hospital where he was subjected to "electromagnetic microwave technology" that caused him to hear voices. No judge would buy this – or would they?

Marcus has done a really thorough job in drafting the complaint. He cited cases and law; and if I didn't know better, I might think he had a decent case. The complaint accuses me of "encouraging" him to sign himself into the hospital. That's not against the law, right?

Bubbles. My blood bubbles in the way that all liquids do before they come to a complete boil and begin to overflow. How can this man, who I gave everything for, still want to take something more? Skimming through the document again, I see that Marcus is demanding one billion dollars in damages. Well, if that doesn't make him look crazy, I don't know what will.

Choked with emotion and utterly confused about how to react, I call Lela.

"Hey, girl," Lela says in a soothing but rushed tone. "You sound like something's up. Are you ok? I thought we agreed not to worry about the test. Is it still bothering you?"

"Uh, no . . . I'm sorry to bother you at work. It's just that I got something new to worry about. I called you because the craziness just won't end . . . He's suing me, Lela." I bite my lower lip as I attempt to center myself.

Lela can't hold in a gasp. "Wha-a-a-t? Who's suing you? For what?"

"Let's see here . . . The plaintiff is suing me for 'encouraging him to check in to a mental hospital, where they conducted electromagnetic microwave technology on him that caused him to hear voices' . . ."

"You're kidding me, right? That's insane. Completely and totally insane."

"Yeah, I know, but there's no mistaking his intent. He's asking for one billion dollars . . . "

"Wait, did you say a billion, with a *b*?"

"Yep, you heard me right. Even though Marcus shouldn't have a case, he could try to drag this out. I'm so tired of dealing with him and all this mess. I take one step forward and he pulls me right back." I exhale, trying to relieve some of the tension building behind my eyes.

"Ok, I can see why you might feel that way, but there's more to it than that. Girl, this situation has been worse than anything I could imagine, but you also have to know that it's not really Marcus doing these crazy things. In his right mind, he'd never do anything like this. Right?"

"I don't know anymore." I glance upward and sigh as my mind considers what my friend has just pointed out.

"Angie?" Lela says gently.

"Well, ok, you're right. The man I married treated me like a queen. He didn't have a vindictive bone in his body – at least none that I ever saw."

"So you just have to keep that in mind when your emotions overwhelm you. This is not Marcus."

I pause, still confused about what to do next. "But do you think I should try to talk to him about it? Reason with Marcus?"

"For what?" Lela questions, then laughs at the futility of the idea. "From what I've heard from you, as well as seen myself, he's not really hearing anything right now."

"But what if I can't get this dismissed? What if we get some crazy judge who wants to make sure that Marcus is getting a fair shot? You know as well as I do that some judges do that. They go out of their way to make sure that there's not some kernel of truth to the claims. Even the whacky ones."

Never one to mince words, Lela quickly jumps in to make her point. "Ok, so I get that you're worried about losing the case, right? Although I think that's extremely far-fetched. But if you want to really think this through, consider this: Do you have a billion dollars?" she asks innocently.

"Of course not." I was becoming annoyed at the obvious.

"Then why in the world are you worried?"

Much as I wanted to hold on to my scowl, my hard exterior cracks and a giggle escapes involuntarily. I laugh for a moment, then stop suddenly.

"I just want this to be over. For once and for all, I just want to be done with this. I'm just tired of him making me feel so bad all the time."

"Well, Angie, you can't control him, but you can control you. You may have to change in a way that doesn't allow him to control how you feel."

But how can he not affect me? Here I was, minding my own business and trying really hard to get back to a normal life. Instead, I have to worry about lawsuits, and worse, about my HIV test results.

When will it end?

39

MAYBE I SHOULDN'T HAVE TAKEN THE TEST, I think, then quickly dismiss the thought as I consider never knowing my HIV status. I took the test so I can face the truth. No more living in fear.

I try to appear calmer than I feel, as I sit in the clinic awaiting my results. But, my bouncing leg probably gives me away. Up and down it goes, hell-bent on speaking its truth. I can't stop my mind from thinking that at any given minute the door will open and my life will either continue as I know it, or will take a drastic turn. How would I deal with a positive result?

After at least twenty minutes, the door finally opens, and in walks my future in the form of a young, blondish, skinny white girl, who doesn't look a day over twenty-two. How can someone so young tell me anything?

The girl smiles at me, but I don't have the energy to smile back. My leg comes to an abrupt stop, my heart slows, and my mouth grows dry. I am sorry I didn't let Lela come with me.

Fortunately, she doesn't waste time with small talk.

"Good news. Your test results show that you're HIV negative." She smiles and waits for a response.

I just sit there, waiting for the warm rush of energy and relief to rush over me, as the girl explains that I should take another test at least six months out from my last sexual contact. Why am I not jumping up and down and doing a happy dance? I am happy and I am certainly relieved, but I guess I expected to feel more. Somehow I'd expected a good report to erode the negative feelings that were consuming me. Instead, all I feel is anger: anger at Marcus, at myself, and most of all, at God.

I quickly pick up my bag and mutter a quick thanks to the girl, while heading toward the door.

40

I'VE BEEN SITTING IN THE SAME SPOT ON THE EDGE of the bed in Lela's guest room for at least an hour – since Lela and Derek left for Wednesday night church service. The room is completely dark, save the light that filters in under the closed door, and the house is so quiet that I feel as if I can't help but to hear myself think. That's when I hear the voice I've come to know and trust.

It's time for you to go home.

Though I'd rather go almost anywhere else, after a few weeks of hiding, I know the voice is right. I've been running too long. Time to face my life, and deal with the madness instead of waiting for it to magically disappear.

Although I have absolutely no clue what I'll do when I get there, I quickly pack my belongings, moving swiftly for fear that if I hesitate, I might change my mind. I really don't want to go.

After so much time away from home, I expected to have a plan. But I don't. All I know is that it's time.

I take a few minutes to write a thoughtful note of gratitude to Lela and Derek for opening their home, and place it on the breakfast table. Then I throw my bags into the back of the truck and hop in.

Much too soon for my liking, I am back at home. Staring at the rust-colored door that leads back into my old life. Wondering if this is a good idea after all.

Balancing the luggage on one side, I struggle to unlock the door without losing my balance. What I see and hear when I finally get the door open throws me completely off guard.

Melodic sounds of smooth jazz and the flickers of several candles greet me as I enter the front room. Marcus is perched on the couch with his freshly shaved head laid back – the seeming picture of relaxation. Except for his weight loss, he looks much like he did before everything started. It used to be routine for him to come home from work and put on soft music to unwind. From time to time, we'd sit together for an hour or more without saying a word. Just being and enjoying a moment.

It only takes that little bit of nostalgia to melt all the grief and anger that has been mounting inside me. I start to pray that maybe, just maybe, the man I knew is still here . . . somewhere.

"Hey, sweetie . . . I'm back," I say tentatively. I take a few steps farther into the room and try to figure out what to say next.

"I . . . uh . . . well, I missed you." I don't care how weak it sounds. Even after everything we've been through, I still love him more than anything.

There is a brief pause during which I wonder if he heard me. But before I can repeat myself, he speaks.

"Hello, Angela."

It is a voice I don't recognize. Not one of anger, but certainly not excitement to mirror my own emotions. It is then that I notice his eyes. Still the same soft brown pools that I used to dive into, but now they look vacant and cold. Not like I remember. Before.

I am not sure what to say next, but decide that actions speak louder than words. I begin to move toward him, hesitantly, for fear of how he might respond.

"It's really good to see you . . . Is it ok – I mean, uh, well, I haven't seen you in weeks . . . Can I have a hug?" I hate to sound like I am begging, but I put my pride aside.

"No," he replies, without looking at me directly.

Just like that, all of the energy and strength that I built up while gone begins to dissipate. I try to hold it together, but once the tears start, they won't stop flowing. My tears aren't angry or heavy; they are quiet, soft tears that say: There just isn't any more hurt left.

Suddenly the room seems smaller and darker than I remembered. It is as if the walls are closing in on me and I can hardly breathe. It is like going back to jail after being released for a short pardon. Suffocating.

Maybe because I am a glutton for punishment or truly a fool for love, I try again to initiate conversation.

"Maybe I could fix us something to eat? Is there anything you'd like? Just tell me if you want something in particular, 'cause I can always run to the store. Even though it's late, I can still run and pick something up if you want."

Another pause makes me wonder if he is going to respond at all.

"Do whatever the hell you want, Angela . . . Just leave me the hell alone."

Now I am stunned. Not even in our worst moments have we cursed at each other. Who is this man?

"Marcus, I don't know what's up with you, but the cursing isn't cool . . . I was just trying to offer to help you."

"I'll say whatever the hell I want . . . Do you hear me, Angela? I'll talk the way I damn well please in my house."

Though his words are cruel, Marcus' voice never rises above his normal tone. In fact, he barely looks at me while speaking, as if completely uninvolved in our discussion.

My hurt is replaced with anger.

"*Your* house? The one I'm paying for by myself? I don't think you want to go there." I say, hoping that it sounds more confident than I feel. Though I am brimming with anger, I try to keep my voice steady, realizing that perhaps I should be afraid of what this new Marcus might do.

"Are you trying to threaten me?" Marcus sneers at me, and then laughs loudly as if watching a comedic routine. "What are you going to do? Call the police? Tell them 'oooh, my husband cursed at me?' Yeah, I'm sure they'll run right over for that one," he taunts, still laughing. "Besides, we never quitclaimed your name onto the deed when you couldn't make it to the closing. Remember? So the way I see it, this is my house, with my name on the deed, and if you don't like it, you're welcome to go back to wherever the hell you came from, 'cause I don't want you here."

It is as if someone has turned off the tear faucet. In that single moment, and in a way that I probably can never describe to another human soul, I understand the scene in *What's Love Got To Do With It* when Tina Turner finally really sees herself in the mirror. Everything snaps into focus as I suddenly see myself and the situation for what it really is.

Mary was right. The man I knew is gone. And he probably isn't coming back, certainly not in time to save our marriage. I can't run anymore. It is time to look out for me.

"So, you really think the marriage is over?" I ask, still somewhat tentatively, holding my breath and not really sure what response I am hoping for.

"Duh! Of course it's over," he replies. "I already talked to a lawyer."

"A lawyer? When were you going to tell me this?"

Marcus doesn't respond, even though I am glaring at him.

Finally, realizing that he must be done talking, I go into the guest room. With my back against the door, I stand there waiting for the tears to come.

The longer I stand there, however, the more I realize that sadness isn't what I feel. Of course, I hurt for my marriage and for the man I once loved, but above everything else, I am almost ashamed to admit that what I feel is a tiny twinge of relief.

I'm free.

41

SEVEN DAYS LATER, I PUT DOWN A DEPOSIT ON a little cottage for rent in East Atlanta. Exactly two weeks after that, I stand in my family room awaiting movers who will help me start the next phase of the journey.

I am so intent on looking out the window to spot the movers that I don't hear Marcus come into the room.

"You have everything packed?" he asks. His voice is not unkind; instead, it is inquisitive. He sounds like he is talking to a colleague about a business venture.

"Yep," I say. I do not turn to face him.

"Well, I'm going to the library to do some research. So I guess you'll be gone when I get back?"

"Yep." During the past several days I have learned that the trick is to say little and to detach emotionally.

Finally, I glance back at him from the window because I want to see his face one last time. I don't want to fight. Instead, I want one moment of peace to remember the man I have loved for as long as I can remember.

Marcus' face is a portrait of confusion. He looks unsure of what to say, and if I didn't know better, I'd swear his eyes are watering.

"Angie?" He says, his voice faltering.

"Yeah?"

"I'm sorry."

Before I can think of what, if any, response is appropriate, he walks out the door. I don't know if Marcus just had a moment of clarity, or if he even knew what he was saying. Does it even matter?

I'm sorry too, sweetie. I'm sorry too.

Home again, home again, jiggity jig. That's the nursery rhyme line my grandmother used to say when returning from a long trip safely. For whatever reason, that's the phrase that replays in my mind as I drive down Glenwood Avenue, with the movers following closely behind.

This is my new home. Though it is exactly what I want – a rehabbed rental house with a large porch and lots of character – I can't quite imagine what my life will be like here all alone.

Turning into my new driveway, I see two cars are already parked in front. The first car belongs to Lela, but the second one I don't recognize. Maybe it is the Landlord, or one of my utility providers?

Moments later, I see three women coming from the back of the house. Neighbors? In my backyard?

As I get out of the car and the women come closer, I scream out in surprise and glee.

"En-di-a!!!!!!!!!!!!! Chris!!!!!!! Oh my God!!! Oh my God!"

I have to resist the urge to break into a full-fledged run that would rival the scene in *The Color Purple* when the sisters were reunited. But that's exactly how I feel when I recognize Endia and Christine walking toward me with Lela. Like a missing piece has finally been returned.

As I embrace each of them tightly, I can barely form coherent words.

"Wha-a-a-at . . . ? Ho-o-o-o-w . . . ? Y'all know what I'm trying to say! I can't believe you're here. How'd you do this?"

Endia's eyes sparkle mischievously as she adjusts her colorful head wrap, while Christine, after another burst of laughter, starts to answer the question.

"Angie, it wasn't that hard. You told me when you were moving, so I called Endi 'cause we figured you'd need a hand. We didn't bother telling you because we knew you'd try to talk us out of it."

"But how'd you know where to find me?"

As soon as the words are out of my mouth, I remember that Endia asked me a series of questions about Lela, including where she worked.

"You called Lela, didn't you? All I can say is wow. I never suspected a thing!"

"Well, keep in mind that we wouldn't have had to fly all the way down here if you'd just learn how to call people back. Didn't we warn you that we'd come back if you went missing again?" Endia asks.

"Yeah, yeah, yeah . . . I'm just mad that you made Lela sell me out too . . . Lela, you knew all this time?"

"Hey, I didn't want any part of it, but they beat it out of me!" Lela responds, laughing and obviously already at ease with my friends.

This isn't the first time that I have laughed and cried at the same time, but I swear that it never felt so good. Overflowing with emotion, I think of how alone I felt just moments before, but I'm not alone. Not now and not ever.

"So . . . I take it those are the movers?" Endia motions to the two guys standing at the front curb, looking strangely out of place. "Well . . . unlock the door so I can see what you're moving into! I couldn't see anything from the windows."

"I . . . I just can't believe you guys are here! You're right, I would have tried to talk you out of it, but I'm really, really glad I didn't get the chance," I say, my voice sounding less steady than

I intend. It takes everything in me just to get the sentence out without tearing up again. God, I am tired of crying!

Christine just smiles brightly in return, while taking my arm to lead me up the stairs to the place I now call home. Lela and Endia follow closely behind.

"This is beautiful . . . I love old homes," Christine remarks as she enters and takes in the hardwood floors in the living room.

"Well, it's not anything fancy . . . Only two bedrooms and one bath. But when I saw it . . . this place just felt peaceful. You know? And truth be told, it could have been made of cardboard and I wouldn't have cared, as long as it was all mine."

"I like it a lot. It has a good feeling," Endia says.

"I'm glad you think so, 'cause I've never done anything so impulsive in my life!" I say, with a sense of relief. "I was driving by and saw the "For Rent" sign. They were having an open house and I decided to come in. The next thing you know, I'm writing a check out for the deposit." I laugh at myself as I remember the moment of panic I had after returning home and letting what I'd done sink in. A thousand questions and fears had enveloped me, but I'd decided to stick with my gut. It was, after all, time that I learned to trust myself again.

"So how much stuff did you move from your old house?" Christine asks, as the movers start bringing in boxes and putting them in the rooms where they belong.

"Not a lot. Just the furniture from the guest room, a few appliances, and miscellaneous stuff that was just mine . . . It may sound strange, but I didn't want all of that bad energy from the old house. If I'm moving on, I've got to let go of all that."

"Good for you, babygirl!" Endia says encouragingly. "I think you did the right thing."

"Yeah, I guess I just never thought in a million years that I'd get divorced," I say, still hurting though I know being at the new house will have its benefits. "It never even entered my mind, ya know? I just feel like I'm still in shock or something."

"Well, I'm sure none of us can know exactly how you feel, but I definitely feel for you," Lela says. "So, was Marcus there when you left? Did you two talk any more?"

I consider telling them about the strange and unexpected apology that I still can't make heads or tails of, but I don't feel like going into that. It probably didn't mean anything.

"You know what? . . . I don't even want to talk about him . . . I'm just glad you're all here."

"Me too, chica."

"Enough of the sappy stuff," Endia says. "Let's start unpacking your new home."

Opening the first box, I see that it is full of memorabilia – including everything from wedding photos to CDs. I feel my eyes tear up again.

"God, I'm tired of crying already!" I say, holding up a wedding photo to show the others what the tears are about. "It's just weird to try to divide up a life. I mean, when you take pictures, you never think you may later be deciding who gets custody of the photo album. That's just crazy! Not that Marcus cares now anyway. Most of the time lately, it's been feeling like his emotions are just gone . . . Like he died, leaving his body behind, but still walking and talking like a zombie. And even though I know I did everything I could, I still feel so guilty for leaving him. Isn't that crazy? He cheated on me, sued me, and is divorcing me, yet I'm the one who feels guilty."

As I continue to look through the photos, Christine comes over and drapes an arm around me. "It's going to be ok. It'll just take some time."

Precisely on cue, Endia walks over and gently takes the photo album from my hand. Putting the book of photos back into the box and taping it shut, she picks up the carton and puts it in the hall closet.

"Well, this room's done," she says, smiling. We all laugh at Endia's quick fix to what might have become an even more tense situation.

Taking my light laughter as a sign that she'd been successful in breaking the ice, Endia continues. "Hey, since we've made so much progress, I think we should go out as soon as the movers are done . . . maybe get dinner and go hang out somewhere? I don't know how you Atlanta folks do it, but surely there's someplace we can go to just get out of the house? We've had enough heaviness for one day. I think a night of laughter is just what the doctor ordered."

"What? You? . . . Go out? As in outside?" I feign shock.

"Oh, stop putting me in a box, will you? I go out from time to time . . . I think the last time was 2005, but hey, I do get out," Endia says, joining in the group laughter.

"That's funny, and probably true," I say. "Actually, I could use a change of pace. I can't remember the last time I did something fun . . . Christine, are you in?"

"Girl, please! I'm already dressed and waiting on you."

"Lela?"

"A chance to hang out and play single for a night? Girl, I already told my husband that he'd see me when he sees me . . . I am most definitely in."

"I know the perfect spot," Christine says, with a mischievous grin.

42

APACHE CAFÉ IS A HOLE-IN-THE-WALL HANGOUT that I have seen advertised in a free newspaper listing Atlanta events, but have never before checked out personally. In classic Love Jones style, the cafe has various open mic nights, as well as a strong following of artists.

"This is a cool spot," I say, as we pay our admission and head to the bar to get drinks. I nervously check to make sure the colorful headwrap that Endia lent me is still in place, and silently hope that it somehow distracts from my ill-fitting jeans and plain white shirt. It had taken thirty minutes of Endia going through my luggage to finally realize I wasn't exaggerating when I said I no longer have a night wardrobe.

"Chris, I can't believe you know more about Atlanta than I do. How'd you hear about this place again?"

Chris shrugs her shoulder and says "It's supposed to be the place to go for music. I'm surprised you've never been here."

"Well I feel like I've been in a marriage coma for way too long," Lela says.

Her words remind me that I'm about to be single again and the heaviness threatens to return. I see Endia looking at me, reading my thoughts, and I force myself to smile.

When it is finally our turn to be waited on, a youthful-looking bartender comes to the end where we are standing.

"What will it be?" the barman asks.

"Um . . . hmm . . . I'm not sure," Endia says, speaking up first, though she is the non-drinker in the group. "What do you recommend?"

"Well, it depends on what you're in the mood for. Wine, beer, cocktails . . . We've also got the boring stuff – soda, juice, coffee, teas . . . We've also got mixed drinks, martinis, mojitos . . . What do you think?"

"I think I'll just take a soda," I say. "Or better yet, some hot tea."

"Is this a girls' night out to celebrate?" the bartender asks.

"Well, yeah, I guess you could say that," I say, because I don't feel like explaining.

"Well, then, you can't go out like that!" he says. "You need something a little more festive. Let me hook you up with some Long Island Iced Teas."

"Whoa! . . . Naw, I can't hang with that," I say. "The last time I had a Long Island, the room got blurry." I laugh at the memory from my first year of law school when I'd tried to hang with some new friends from New York who were clearly more friendly with alcohol than I had been. "What else do you suggest?"

"Don't pay her any mind. We'll take one of those iced teas for her," Endia says, in a tone that indicates I shouldn't even bother arguing differently. "I'll have a hot tea, of the boring variety . . . What do you all want?"

After Lela and Christine place and pick up their orders, we find a spot with enough seating near the back exit in an area of sofas and chairs. Quietly, at first, we sip our drinks while taking in the scenery. The clientele appears to be a mixture of folks from age twenty to forty-something, business people to artists, male, female, gay, straight – you name it, and it is here. The live band on stage is playing a jazzy tune, as folks continue to sign up to perform on the mic. It's a great vibe, but I find myself fidgeting.

"It feels kind of weird to be out," I finally say. "Even though this isn't a real meat market kind of place, it's been a long time since I've hung out at any nightspot at all . . . I don't know if I'm really ready for this."

"Ready for what?" Endia asks, gesturing around with her hands. "Friendly conversation? Good music? What do you need to 'be ready' for? . . . Puh-lease. If I can get out of the house, then so can you."

I smile at the simplicity in Endia's words and just shake my head in response.

"Well, I'm just glad the place is cool," Christine says. "I wasn't sure what to expect when I heard about it. A guy I met at the airport mentioned that this is one of Atlanta's hot spots."

"Wait a minute," Endia says, eying her closely. "Not the guy you met at O'Hare this morning? The one I saw you talking to?"

"Yeah, him."

"Nah, it couldn't be the same one . . . because the guy I'm thinking of is the one that we decided you wouldn't call because he just broke up with his fiancée, right?"

And they are off to their usual sparring. I catch something about him not really being available, and a retort about how at least Chris puts herself out there. I lean back and enjoy the normalcy of it all.

Finally when it sounds like it's getting heated, I give Endia a look that says "just let it go," so she doesn't say anything further, but I can see her literally biting her tongue to keep quiet. If Chris wants to keep dating emotionally unavailable men, then that is her choice, right? Honestly, I am just glad to get lost in someone else's drama for a minute.

Thirty minutes later, Marcus is the furthest thing from my mind. Maybe it is because of the drink or perhaps the carefree environment. In fact, I am so engrossed in the music – listening to a local artist named Quinn "doing Carl Thomas" as well as Carl himself – that I don't see the guys approaching our table.

"Christine, hey, I'm glad you made it out."

Chris turns and appears to recognize the guy standing before her. I assume it must be the airport man.

"Ron . . . hi!" Christine says, as she stands up to hug him. "Let me introduce you to my girls. I don't think you really got to meet Endia in the airport this morning, but she's one of my close friends from Chicago. This is Angela, who we're here visiting. We all went to school together at Howard. And this is a new friend – Angela's girl, Lela."

"Ladies, it's nice to meet you . . ." Then gesturing to the two guys who are standing slightly behind him, Ron adds, "This is Allen and this is my man, Kevin."

After exchanging polite greetings, the men sit down. Ron sits next to Christine and Lela on the couch, while Kevin and Allen pull up chairs on either side of the loveseat where Endia and I are sitting.

"So, how do you guys know each other?" Christine asks, having to yell a bit over the music.

All three guys start to speak up at once, but Ron finally takes the lead.

"The three of us go all the way back to high school . . . And you know that's been a minute." He pauses as they all laugh. "Seriously, these are my boys for life . . . Actually, they were supposed to be the best men in my wedding tomorrow . . ."

My eyes lock with Endia. Without speaking, I know she's also hoping Christine hasn't missed the sad look in Ron's eyes when he refers to his wedding. No way this brotha is even close to being ready to meet someone else.

"But it's all good. We're just out for a drink."

Ron is a fairly attractive guy. Probably about five feet eleven inches, with a build that says he likely played football back in the day. Way back in the day. But his boys, Kevin and Allen – I don't know if it's just that I haven't really noticed guys in a long time, but both look *fine*. I haven't gotten a chance to observe Allen's personality, since he is sitting next to Endia farthest away from me, but Kevin seems to have it going on all around. He is probably about six feet one, with a beautiful smile, and the longest eyelashes I have ever seen on a man. More importantly, he has an ease and confidence about him that are as attractive as his exterior.

As conversations seem to break off into subgroups to avoid yelling over the noise, Kevin leans over – a little closer than necessary, I think – and says "Can I get you a drink or something?"

I notice the way his hand grazes my shoulder as he leans in, and I inhale the hint of cologne that lingers even after he sits back in his seat. I can't believe I am sitting here checking out some guy, when I have been separated for mere hours. What's wrong with me?

Realizing he is still waiting for a response, I finally speak up. "Uh, what did you ask?"

As he moves in to speak again, I instinctively shrink back in my seat – suddenly feeling awkward and as if I am in foreign territory. When was the last time a cute guy approached me, or better yet, that I even noticed?

"A drink . . . I was asking if you wanted something else to drink." Kevin looks unsure of how to proceed since I am being so standoffish.

I sit there trying to look more cool than I feel, while wrestling with my discomfort. I miss the ease that Marcus and I developed after knowing each other for so long, and I tense thinking about starting over. How can I ever trust myself again? I don't ever want to hurt again the way I do now. No way. Love is for suckers.

I avoid direct eye contact with Kevin and instead look for the ladies' room. I have to get out of here.

"So, I take that as a no," he says.

"Oh. I, uh, well, I really appreciate that, but I think I'm pretty much past my limit," I finally say.

"Oh, ok . . . So, have you been here before?"

"Uh . . . No, this is my first time."

Suddenly my headwrap seems like a ridiculous charade, and I feel completely out of place. I want to evaporate. *Save your lines for someone who is buying it*, I want to say, but instead opt for something more tactful.

"Look, um . . ."

"Kevin."

"Kevin . . . I'm sure you're a really nice guy," I say, noticing again what a beautiful smile he has.

"Uh-oh, that doesn't sound like a compliment." Kevin shakes his head and laughs.

"Look, really, it's not you . . . But we're here 'celebrating' – if you want to even call it that – my pending divorce, so . . . so, I'm probably not the best company."

"Oh. Wow. Look, I'm really sorry about your divorce," he responds. "I didn't mean to intrude on a girls' night or to make you feel uneasy . . . Anyway, it's all good if you don't feel like talking. I'm just here to look after my boy . . ."

"Well, cool, then I guess we're on the same program . . . Don't laugh, but I was just sitting here praying that you weren't flirting because I'm so not in that place."

Kevin laughs heartily before responding. I join in, but don't know what is so funny.

"Nah, no flirting . . . I think my wife might have a little bit of a problem with that," he says, good-naturedly. "What Ron didn't mention is that he was the best man at my wedding seven years ago."

"Seven years? Wow, that's really great," I say, trying to hide my embarrassment. Now I see the prominent band on his left finger, and wonder how I could have missed it before.

For the next twenty minutes I grow to like Kevin even more as he tells me the story of how he and his wife met, and how he knew she was the one. I am both uplifted and depressed at the same time. Uplifted by hearing that there are men who value love and honor their commitments. Depressed by knowing that I didn't have that kind of relationship and probably never will.

"Hey, Kevin, would you excuse me for a minute? I need to find the ladies' room." I stand up and try to appear more sober than I feel. "Anyone else need the ladies' room?" I ask my girls during a momentary lull in the music.

As if cued to synchronize, Lela and Christine each stand up and follow behind me toward the ladies' room, which is in the very back of the club, while Endia waves us on. I walk as straight as I can, focusing on putting one foot in front of the other.

Once we reach the restroom, we have to wait in line. While standing there, I look back to our section and see Endia, doubled over in laughter. She appears to be having a good time with Allen.

I watch them for a bit longer, anticipating that Endia will soon get to her normal brush-off routine. However, to my huge surprise, I see Endia laugh again and move in closer. Not two minutes later, Endia reaches into her bag, and then hands Allen her card.

I am pleasantly surprised, especially since I know better than anyone that tomorrow is not promised.

43

URPRISE DOESN'T EVEN BEGIN TO DESCRIBE HOW I feel when I see Marcus walking toward me in the park near my office on that beautiful, uncharacteristically warm day.

His dark skin glows against the white cotton ensemble that he wears, topped off with what I like to call "Jesus sandals." From his outfit, to the smile he wears, Marcus epitomizes peace. He looks simply beautiful and his eyes say "welcome home."

As he draws closer, I struggle to contain myself. I want to break out into a full run toward Marcus, but am not sure that would be the best move. Can't wait to tell him how much I've missed him, and to fill him in on all that has happened while he was 'gone.' Will he remember or understand everything? It doesn't matter. None of that matters now.

When we finally get close enough to touch, I have lost the ability to speak. I open my mouth, but can't even get the words out to say "I still love you," or "I've missed you." Marcus seems to experience the same thing, because he doesn't talk either. Instead, we just stand there grinning at each other. It reminds me of our morning ritual. When we used to take a moment to just be. Together.

God, I've missed you so much. Do you know that, Marcus? I'm so sorry I left you. You have to know how much I tried. It just didn't seem like you were ever coming back. But here you are. With me. In this moment.

I am still trying to will my brain to allow spoken words, as Marcus takes another step toward me. Taking my hand in his, he pulls me into a close embrace, then whispers into my ear.

"It's not your fault . . ."

What is he talking about? I will the words to come out, but only manage to raise my eyebrows in confusion.

"It's not your fault, baby . . . This is just how it was supposed to be."

Still unable to talk, I open my mouth to respond, then hold up my hands to gesture that I don't understand.

"I'll always love you," he says, while staring at me intently.

I beg him with my eyes to say more, while my arms tighten around him. He smells so good, just like I remember. The perfect combination of Lever soap and his favorite cologne. I find my favorite spot – right in the nook of his neck – and just rest there, inhaling.

The nightmare is finally over.

"Angie . . . Angie! Can you hear me?" Christine's voice sounds miles away.

"Angie, wake up, sweetie." Endia sounds louder and more serious.

After I am finally able to open my eyes, it takes me a moment to get my bearings.

Where am I?

Slowly, I recognize the comforter on my bed and realize that I am in my new bedroom. Looking toward the foot of my bed, I see Christine and Endia, both watching me with concerned expressions.

"Babygirl, we came in to check on you since it's almost noon and no one had heard you up," Endia says. "You were talking loudly in your sleep. Were you dreaming?"

I sit up all the way and pull the covers up under my chin, a pensive look on my face. There is a pause before I say anything more, as I analyze what just happened.

"I guess I was . . . I was dreaming about Marcus. Only it wasn't Marcus the way he is now. It was the way I think Marcus would be if he was better."

"That sounds like a good dream. Go on," Christine says.

"So, he looked . . . incredible . . . Happy and light," I say. "Even though I couldn't talk to him — 'cause it seemed like my mouth wouldn't move or something weird — it was just wonderful being in his space and feeling as if he were ok.

"Now before you guys think I've lost it completely, 'cause I'm both crying and smiling, let me say something. I know that Marcus may never choose to get help — may never look like the Marcus that I saw in my vision. But I still feel that it was God's way of showing me that he's going to be ok. Even if Marcus never physically heals, his spirit is just as beautiful as what I saw. More than that, God gave me a moment to say good-bye in a way that I never could have in person . . . I know it doesn't make much sense, but I have been praying for closure, and I feel like that's exactly what I got. God may not have let my mother's dream come true — for us to have a marriage ministry — but slowly and surely, he's giving me peace . . . In fact, Marcus even told me that he loved me and that it wasn't my fault the way things turned out." I pause to dab the tears at the corners of my eyes, while continuing to smile.

"I still don't understand it all, but feeling like Marcus is in good hands just makes it easier than feeling as if I left him when he was down."

247

"So sweetie, are you really ok?" Endia asks with knowing eyes.

I look up as if saying a silent prayer, then slowly nod my head as I smile more genuinely than I have in a very long time. It may be a while before it doesn't hurt anymore, but finally, I feel a stirring of peace to come.

44

ASING UP TO THE CURB ADJACENT TO THE entrance for ticketing, I think about how different this airport drop-off is compared TO THE ONE BEFORE. Instead of the fear that consumed me back when Marcus first had the breakdown, this time my fear is overshadowed by an excitement about the next phase of my life. No, things sure didn't turn out the way I hoped and planned, but I am going to be ok.

"Angie, you know we're just a phone call away if you need anything, right?" Christine says, while pulling her rolling bag from the trunk. "And don't forget that you promised to come visit us in a few months after you get settled."

"No way, I said I'd come visit in the summer," I say. "You know the rules. You come here during the fall, winter, and your so-called spring. I go there during the summer. No way I'm trying to brave a Chicago winter!"

As both women laugh, Christine pulls me in for a warm embrace, then kisses me on the cheek. "You're going to be just fine, you know."

"I know, and I appreciate you just for being here . . . Call and let me know you made it safely."

"Ok," Christine says, while stepping into the line for curb-side check-in.

I turn to Endia and she pulls me in closely. As we embrace, Endia speaks softly into my ear. "I am so incredibly proud of you."

"What? . . . Why?" I pull back to see Endia's face to try to decipher the meaning in her words.

"Babygirl, I don't even know where to begin!" Endia tells me, with her eyes watering slightly. "I'm proud of you for loving even through the worst of it . . . For showing me by example that love is worth the risk . . . For being stronger than I could have ever been. And just for being you."

"Whoa, you're giving me way too much credit," I say. "You don't know how many nights I cried – or how close I got to just throwing in the towel. Literally. I'm not nearly as strong as you are, Endi."

"Now that's where you're wrong," Endia says. "Being strong doesn't mean you don't cry, or that you don't think about giving in. It just means that every day you pick yourself back up again. That's what you're doing. You're being bold enough to keep loving, even though you got a raw deal last time. Look at you – you're going through a divorce, but still encouraging me with Allen –"

"Oooh, Allen!" I say, mocking Endia's tone, while giggling.

"Whatever, chica . . . Allen really seems like a nice guy . . . and we stayed up all night on the phone talking. Some of the stuff we have in common just feels like our meeting couldn't have been a coincidence." Endia smiles and shrugs her shoulders. "I don't know. Maybe he'll end up just being a good friend."

"Yeah, well, saying my good friends' names doesn't make me smile like that," I say, laughing. "Let's see how I look when I say the name 'Endia.'" I pause dramatically before continuing. "Nope, I got nothing. Not even a tiny grin. But what happens when I say the name 'Allen?'"

Endia rolls her eyes and shakes her head, but not before I see her face.

"Oh my God, you're blushing! Oh . . . my . . . God!"

"Anyway . . . " Endia says, trying unsuccessfully not to smile. "I've got to get moving . . . So you know the drill. You'd best answer your phone from now on so we don't have to come back again."

The two of us hug one last time. Then I get back into the car and drive away without once looking back.

Once on the highway, I put my earpiece in and press "1," then "talk," on my cell phone. Two rings later and I hear a familiar greeting on the other end.

"Hey, baby, how are you today?"

"I'm good, Mom. I just wanted to hear your voice."

"Well, here it is."

We laugh in unison at the familiar joke. It feels good to talk without all the recent tension.

"Mom, can I ask you something?"

"Of course. What is it?" she asks.

"Well . . . Remember when you told me about the dream you had about me and Marcus?"

"Yes, of course."

"Do you still think it was from God? I mean, since it didn't turn out the way you dreamed it?"

"Now why do you say it didn't turn out the way I dreamed it? Just because you and Marcus didn't end up together?"

"Well, yeah. I still remember your words. You said that God said he was going to bring us to a place of brokenness, but that because of it, I'd be stronger. And our marriage would be a ministry."

"But baby, I never said you and Marcus were going to stay married."

"But you said our marriage would be a ministry."

"Yep, and I still think that. I think that because of this, you're going to be able to minister to others who go through something traumatic like you did. Whether it's mental illness or some other unexpected tragedy, you're going to help people know that they can make it through . . . Your life is a ministry . . . Don't you see?"

I am silent as I process my mother's words.

"So do you think that's why this happened to us? So that I can help someone else? I guess maybe that's as good a reason as any, but sometimes I still get so frustrated 'cause I don't really understand."

Now it is my mother's turn to grow silent.

"Mom, you still there?"

"Yeah, I'm sorry. I was just thinking of how to word it . . . I guess I don't really know why this happened, and maybe we'll never fully understand. And God knows I still pray that Marcus will get better. But . . . I look at you now – at the strength I hear in your voice and in your spirit – and I know that you are better because of what you've been through."

I hear my mom's voice crack slightly before she continues.

"Of course I can't say that I liked seeing you go through something like this. But when I look at you now and see how much you've grown, it just warms my heart and somehow makes it ok.

"So, I don't know if this was for your growth, or for someone else's growth, or both. I guess I'm just believing that it will all work out for the good. The sooner you start believing that, and stop being angry, the sooner you can really move on, too."

"Mama, how did you know I was angry?"

"Child, please, haven't I known you for twenty-nine years?" Her mother chuckles, then continues. "Anyway, the next time you get married . . ."

"Next time?" I ask, interrupting my mother. "Whoa, I don't know about all that. I . . ."

"The next time you get married," my mother interjects, sounding confident of her premonition, "you'll cherish every single moment 'cause you'll know that each day is a gift. Whether it's for a season or a lifetime, it's still just as precious."

That night before I go to sleep, I thank God for all of the moments and seasons with Marcus, and ask him to let my life help someone else. And in that single moment, I feel my anger lessen, if only just a bit.

EPILOGUE

45

"COME IN, COME IN," MARY SAYS, THEN GIVES ME a quick hug before waving me in to her office. It feels as warm as it did when I was last here almost a year ago, and Mary's energy feels like coming home.

"You look great," she says, after taking in everything from my highlighted micro-braids to the fullness of my cheeks and the wideness of my smile.

"I feel great," I say, happy that it is true.

"So, I know you said you just wanted to drop something off, but do you have a minute? I'd love to catch up." Mary gestures to a seat across from her and I sit down to share all she has missed. I speak quickly since I don't have much time.

I tell Mary how I finally left Marcus last January, and how we were divorced by April. During that time my feelings went back and forth between relief, hurt, and anger. It was like mourning the death of someone who was still alive. Every time I thought I'd made progress, I'd hear from him or hear stories of him, and I'd go back to ground zero.

But with the passing of time, the weight grew lighter. Finally the day came when I didn't feel as empty and when I was able to pray for Marcus without feeling any heaviness. My sources told me that he moved back to D.C. to stay with a cousin and that he still denies anything is wrong. Unfortunately, the sources also said that he still talks to people who aren't there and spends his time suing people who are part of the conspiracy against him. Yet I haven't given up hope on him finding healing for himself. As long as there is prayer, there is hope.

The good news is that my second HIV test came back negative and I managed to get the lawsuit against me dropped with the help of some of my colleagues. With all of the monumental issues resolved, all that was left was the basic task of learning to be comfortable all alone. That one took more time than I care to admit. Even little things like eating in a restaurant or going out alone had been so scary the first few times. I'd had to make new single friends and to get used to being without a 'plus one.' I'd also had to figure out how to make decisions alone, something I'd grown unaccustomed to doing since Marcus had always been there.

Strangely enough, once I got the hang of it, I began to love my solitude. In fact, when I leave Mary's office I'm headed to the airport for a solo getaway celebration in Aruba. Before, I would have never traveled alone. But now, I'm looking forward to it.

Finally, I tell Mary that the most significant change is that I might finally be ready to give love another try. I still think Marcus was a soulmate, but maybe he was just sent for a season. Maybe this whole experience was just to teach me that love is a precious gift, like my mom said. It doesn't always come when we want it to, and it sometimes leaves before we're ready; but while it's there – whether it's for a moment or a lifetime – we should enjoy it to the fullest. Certainly, if I ever find it again, I'll fight just as hard to see it through, because it's worth it.

I glance at my watch and see that it's already past nine, and I need to hurry this up so I don't miss my flight. Mary is still just as easy to talk to as she was before, and I make a mental note to schedule a real appointment with her when I get back. Never hurts to go in for a tune up before something breaks down.

"Mary, I've really got to run, but before I do, I wanted to give you this," I say, pulling a book out of my bag.

"When I Was Broken," she reads. Mary gives me a questioning look, then smiles at the angel art on the front cover and the author's name. She flips it over and quickly reads the summary on the back.

"You wrote this book?" Mary asks, her tone excited. "Wow, this is incredible."

I bask in the praise, still marveling over the fact that I actually wrote and self-published a book. I'd always wanted to write but never before had a subject I was passionate enough about to see it through.

"What prompted this?" Mary asks.

"A few weeks after I moved into my new place, the weirdest thing happened to me," I began. For the next several minutes, I fill Mary in on my real life encounter with an angel.

I was working late one night when one of the cleaning crew members came into my office to dust. It caught me a bit off guard because in all my time there, I'd never before seen this woman. In fact, I barely saw any of the cleaning crew because they usually worked in the wee hours, and it was not yet even eight.

The woman, Faith, was an African-American woman of average height and weight, brown skin, and no real distinguishable characteristics. There wasn't anything unusual about her, yet for some unknown reason, I felt drawn to her. I watched her out of the corner of my eye for several minutes, then finally followed my gut and casually asked how she was doing.

After making small conversation for a few minutes, I saw her take a deep breath as if summoning up her courage. She walked over close to my desk and in a soft, trembling voice asked "do you know where I can get a divorce if I don't have much money?"

I thought it was a weird coincidence that she would ask me that, but then shook it off because, after all, divorce is pretty common. Opting to help her, I logged onto the internet to pull up the numbers for some resources, while mentioning that I was going through a divorce and understood how hard it could be.

259

That's when it got really bizarre. The woman looked at me, with glistening eyes, and said, "My situation is a little different. You see, my husband is schizophrenic and I just don't know if I can leave him. I can't leave him if he's sick, can I?"

At that point, I felt as if time stood still. I felt as if it couldn't be an accident that I worked late on a night when this woman came into my office.

"She asked you that?" Mary asks in an excited tone, moving to the edge of her seat. "Are you kidding me?"

I shake my head to indicate that every word is true.

"You're telling me that a stranger just happened to come into your office, without knowing anything about you or your situation, and asked you for advice on a divorce from a schizophrenic man?"

I nod, realizing how crazy the story sounds even though I witnessed it first-hand.

"Unbelievable. Truly unbelievable," Mary finally says. Then after a few seconds, "So, what did you tell her?"

At this question, I have to smile. What could I have possibly told her except the wise words that someone once said to me?

"I told her that there comes a time when you have to protect yourself," I say. "I told her that if she was being abused, under any definition, she needs to get out of there. Finally, I told her that even when you love someone, sometimes you have to let go."

Then, after I finished telling her, I wrote a book about my experience, knowing that there are thousands of women out there who need to hear the same.

God brought me to a place of brokenness, but through it he made me stronger. And he allowed my marriage to be a ministry for others.

For that, I am eternally grateful.

THE END

Reader's Guide Questions

1. Angela believed in the notion of "forever love" and in "soulmates." Do you?

2. What do you think about Angela's decision to stay and fight for her marriage? Do you consider her character to be weak or strong?

3. If your spouse cheated, would you attempt to repair what was broken in your marriage?

4. What are acceptable grounds for divorce?

5. Do we talk enough about mental health issues in our community?

6. Should patients be allowed the right to refuse medical treatment and/or medication if they are not a danger to themselves or others?

7. Can God reveal things to people in dreams?

8. Have you ever felt broken?

9. There's an old saying that "what doesn't kill you, makes you stronger." True or false?

10. In the end of the book, Angela found a place of wholeness and learned to do more things alone. Should she have learned this earlier? How important is this for singles and/or for those in relationships?

Author's Note

Sometimes it seemed like this book would NEVER come to fruition! It all began more than a decade ago when I prayed for God to give me a story.

And, He did.

Though it took longer than expected to birth, I always knew this story was meant to be told – for every person who has been touched by mental health issues, and as importantly, for anyone who has ever known what it feels like to have life take an unexpected turn. I'm here to tell you that the greatest challenges can turn into the biggest blessings.

There's no way I can thank everyone to whom I owe a debt of gratitude. So before even attempting to list names, let me just say a heartfelt thank you to every person who gave me a kind word as I was going through and every person who never tired of asking me "how's the book coming?" even when I gave a weary shrug in response. This book came to be because of you.

Ok, here goes nothing (please, please "blame it on my head and not my heart" if you're not listed here):

A special thank you to my sisters Janice, Joyce, and Lela (for never ceasing to pray); Erika D., Joy D., Lisa H., Tamara G., and Crystal N. (my other "sisters"); Dee, Desh, Kat, Kaye, Kinaya, LaTanga, Shantell, and Tanisa – with shouts out to Tanisa and Tangie for their editing skills and to Dee for designing my beautiful website (for showing me that love is boundless); Deb,

265

Faith, Karol, La Tonya, Leslie L., Nina, and Tammy (for being my "legends"); Tanya H., Tralonda, Naomi, Kareem D., Greg R., Quinn, Wendy G., Joy H., Marcus B., Monica P., Stephanie C., Katrina T., Tia, Ron F., Von P., Kyle W., Doral, Dex, Mark N., Marc S., Norbert, Regina W., Lance D., Andrea D., Tara T., Beth, Dion, Nicole G., Linda W., and Kefentse – with a special shout-out to Tara for her invaluable comments, (because I am so thankful God placed you in my path); Leslie T., Annette, and Dr. Mary (angels who appeared at the right time); Chad (for teaching me the meaning of the word "friend"); Tin Man (for reminding me I have a heart); Obi (for confirming there's such a thing as "soulmates").

More Than A Bookclub – with special shouts out to Christine, Kara, and Angela (for your unending support); Travis Hunter, Sherri Lewis, Dr. Maiysha Clairborne, Jay White, Tina McElroy Ansa, Nea Simone, Tananarive Due, Reshonda Tate, and the Authority Writing Group – with special shouts out to Kellyn, Lashana, and Rod (for helping me believe that I'm a writer and for reading many, many drafts); Jo-Ann Langseth (for professionally editing one of my final drafts); George I. Crawford (for his incredible photography skills used for the book cover), and La Tonya Williams (again – for stepping in at the 9th hour to create my beautiful book cover and just for being there).

And, to my soulmate/twin-flame/life partner . . . I still believe.

Finally, at the risk of making this waaaaayyyyy too long (as if it isn't already), I must add a special thanks to my mother, who transitioned from this earth the day after I sent this book to print. There are no words to embody what she meant to me, or to describe how her strength (even in her weakness) helped me grow. I'll miss the way she said so much in so few words . . . I'll miss her strawberry cakes and mouth-watering gumbo. . . . But I'll rest in knowing she is finally at peace and never far from me. And, I'll hold on to the picture of her and my Daddy reunited in heaven. ☺

I love you Mommy and Daddy. Hope I am making you both proud.

Peace and blessings,

Imani

About The Author

Since receiving a journalism degree from the University of Texas at Austin, and a law degree from Howard University, Imani has written and edited numerous works, including a book of inspirational thoughts, entitled YOU ARE NOT ALONE (2009). An attorney by trade, Imani is also a life coach and speaker, dedicated to inspiring others to live each moment to the fullest.

To keep up to date with Imani's events and to subscribe to her blog, please visit www.byimani.com.